DEDICATION

This book is dedicated to my friend Barbara, who was my best friend in high school and still continues to amaze me as an adult. For all the true events of our shared past that inspired this work of fiction I say thank you. I hope that someday we will live close enough to each other to have daily experiences like we did in high school! By the way, she was taller and blonder than me. Remember the apples!

THANK-YOUS

I want to thank my agent, Steve, who said, "Why don't you write a book?" He's a real "you can do it" kind of guy and for that faith I am extremely grateful.

If there was a word that meant I get to be friends with the "coolest, most inspiring person I could ever imagine," I would use that word in CAPITAL letters to describe my friend Amy. Then if there was a word that meant "thank you for being such an important part of my creative energy," I would use that word next. I would put those two words together and she would know how much she means to me. Then I would say, "Hey, I like your shoes!" because she always has great shoes.

(Chapter 1)

MONDAY

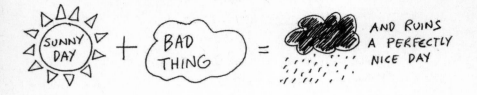

it's completely unfair that bad things happen on sunny days.

SUNNY DAY + BAD THING = AND RUINS A PERFECTLY NICE DAY

The Sarahs (my friends at school—Sarah W. And Sarah J.) are mad because I had lunch with Sandra (my 24-hour friend) instead of them. They had some big, exciting news to share with me, but I already had plans to eat lunch with Sandra, so I missed out on what it was. A normal person would just have lunch with everybody, but Sandra and the Sarahs don't mix well—imagine tuna fish mixed with ice cream. I tried to meet up with them after school to find out the news, but they ignored me. I saw them down the street and yelled, but they pretended not to hear me and kept walking. I hate stuff like that. It's exactly what Mom does to Dad to make him miserable. When things like that happen in your home life, you are extra sensitive to it in the outside world. It has an extra sting!

TUNA FISH SALAD

ICE CREAM

YUCK

GOT YOU ON A WEAK SPOT! HA! HA!

On top of that, Mom seemed to be in one of her I-have-no-friends funks. She's been awfully moody ever since Aunt Chester moved away—FOUR YEARS AGO! You'd think she'd be over it by now. Aunt Chester is not her real name. It's Emily, like mine, but in high school her bazoombas suddenly inflated "like a life raft off a sinking ship"—Dad's saying—and the name just stuck. That's the scary thing about nicknames—the sticking factor.

Aunt Chester went to school with Dad (she's not my real aunt), and they were best friends until she met Mom. Dad says, "She dropped me like a hot potato and joined Camp Adna." Adna is Mom's name. Dad says lots of things that cause my eyes to roll up—it's completely conscious!

Mom and Aunt Chester are "soul-mate friends." Usually people marry their soul mates, but Mom married Dad, so she has a soul-mate friend instead. They can tell in the first three seconds of a phone call if everything is okay or not, just by the hellos. Sometimes they even seem psychic. Like the time Mom couldn't find her silver hoop earrings, which she almost never wears. She was just about to accuse me of taking them, giving me her I'll-get-the-truth-out-of-you stare, like I would wear them for anything other than dressing up as a pirate or a gypsy for Halloween, when the phone rang. It was Aunt Chester saying she'd found Mom's earrings under the bed.

Anyway, that's why it wasn't so completely weird that right when I was wishing something good would happen—because nothing good or exciting ever happens, and you don't wish for something you already have—my birthday present from Aunt Chester arrived (my birthday was three months ago). Aunt Chester is like that—she has unpredictably good timing. Wishing for something and having follow-through on that wish hardly ever happens, so when it does it's really something you should take notice of.

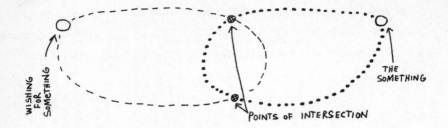

WISHING FOR SOMETHING

THE SOMETHING

POINTS OF INTERSECTION

I love the UPS man—like I love Santa Claus but without the pretend part. After the UPS guy left, Mom just stood there, in the doorway, staring off into space. Like she was waiting for another package or wished she could have gone with him or something. He wasn't even the regular kind-of-good-looking one. I finally had to do that hand thing where you snap your fingers to say, "Come on let's have it." After all it was MY package! And did she hand it over? No! Instead she gave me one of her famous mega sighs, because she wanted me to say, "Oh, what's wrong? Are you okay?" which I didn't because I'm selfish and wanted to open my present instead of listening to her complain. And I know that mega sighs always, always, always lead to long, drawn-out tales of sadness and martyrdom—at least in our house.

Finally she held it out and said, "Good things come in small packages." She's not big on clichés, so I could tell she was distracted and baking some kind of nut dessert or mad at Dad, an almost weekly ritual. (They both seem to take about the same amount of grumpy energy.) She only bakes stuff with nuts because she is allergic to them. It's her own insane weight-loss plan—her sacrifice so the rest of the family can have a dessert that she can't eat, even if she wanted to. It's sad. She has absolutely no willpower.

Anyway, I gave her a super-cheery "thanks" and ran up to my room. Sometimes the best way to battle a grump is to fight back with over-the-top niceness. It really annoys them (very satisfying!).

Generally, I'm kind of a big-package person. Small packages are for girls who like shiny silver lockets, ankle bracelets, or sparkly earrings, and I come from "a long line of non-jewelry-wearing females." That's what Mom always says every time Dad hands her a big, badly wrapped box (he believes in speed wrapping over quality wrapping) on her birthday or Christmas. She could be a little more upbeat . . . at least he tries. My friend Becca's dad doesn't even give out presents, except to their dog, Monte.

Enough Mom and Dad complaining. (It could potentially fill an encyclopedia—and who's got time to write one of those?) It was present time! I pulled it out of the box. A box wrapped in recycled wrapping paper. "Recycled" as in used for someone else's present. Lots of fold lines and bits of paper missing from pulled tape—kind of a disappointment. Aunt Chester is a little too thrifty. I opened the card. I always open cards first. They're like the instruction manual for the present. For example . . .

"Just a little something"

and

"I've always wanted you to have this"

mean entirely different things. Like my friend Sandra says, "Car keys don't come with a 'just a little something' card." Not that I'm expecting car keys—at least not yet. Aunt Chester's card was, surprise, a cow card; this time a cow in an art museum wearing a beret and admiring a painting of a haystack. French cow or wanna-be artist cow? She's always sending me cow cards. I don't even like cows. Big mammals kind of freak me out. Why does she think this is funny? Obviously weird funny, not ha-ha funny (very different). Thankfully, she doesn't send "joke" presents too!

This time, her card was a giveaway.

> *Dear Emu,*
> *I thought you might like to give these a try —*
> *A fun journaling project!*
> *Love, Aunt Chester*

> NOTE: AUNT CHESTER IS THE ONLY PERSON IN THE WHOLE WORLD WHO CALLS ME EMU. DAD ONCE TRIED, BUT I DIDN'T TALK TO HIM FOR TWO DAYS AND MOM GAVE HIM THE WHAT FOR SO HE STOPPED. EMUS HAVE BEADY, BLACK EYES AND LONG LEGS—I WOULDN'T MIND HAVING LONGER LEGS.

Aunt Chester has been keeping a journal since she was eight years old. She has boxes and boxes of them. She says it gives her life perspective, which she says is the difference between watching a movie and being in a movie. Which kind of makes sense.

JOURNAL LOGIC (WATCHING)
VS.
NON-JOURNAL LOGIC (BEING)

TYPE OF MOVIE	WATCHING THE MOVIE	BEING IN THE MOVIE
HORROR	You would never in a million years go down into the basement alone.	You walk into the basement alone to check out the strange noise.
COMEDY	You would always cover up before answering the door.	You answer the door in your ratty underpants because you are sure it's just your mom, but it's the UPS man and your very hot English teacher instead.
ROMANCE	You would know that the extra-hot popular guy is really shallow so you wouldn't even give him the time of day.	You give your heart to the extra-hot popular guy and he uses it and throws it away like a wipe.

Aunt Chester says, "Anything that helps you make fewer mistakes in life is a good idea." According to Dad, her life is "rife with drama"—something about having too many boyfriends and no husband (sounds good to me). So who knows what would have happened to her if she hadn't kept all those journals. Maybe she'd be married and completely unhappy. She gave me my first journal last year. At first, I didn't know what to write about. What I was wearing? School? What the POKs (Popular Obnoxious Kids) look like when you are sure they are talking about you?

Too much work!

I was going to save it until something exciting happened, but Aunt Chester made me promise to write just four sentences a day. After a while, it seemed like I was always writing about the same stuff, so I stopped. Whenever she asks about it I say, "I'm still working on it," and then change the subject. It's one of those make-someone-else-feel-good lies—the kind that don't really count. I know she wants me to like the journal thing as much as she does, but my life is not as exciting as hers (no boyfriend).

Hoping it wasn't another blank book—how many journals does one girl need?—I ripped the present open. I'm the only one in my family who rips wrapping paper. Everyone else uses a knife and carefully pries off the tape, like they're doing present surgery. It's a real downer during holidays. It was a box of cards: "Flashcards of My Life—Cards All About You." At first I thought the cards would be all filled out—sort of a "read all about Emily" thing. Reading nice things about yourself is the greatest, and it's only second best to hearing nice things about yourself. Like if people think you are asleep or in another part of the house and they are talking about you. But when I looked at the cards, they were all blank. Another project where I'd have to do all the work. Great! (Sarcastic.)

BOX

SAMPLE CARD

(Other side is blank)

Not the best present I ever got, but still . . . maybe if I wrote big and flashy, I could fill them out pretty quickly.

HANDWRITING SAMPLE

BIG AND FLASHY	*Emily Rules*
NORMAL	Emily is OK

Knowing Aunt Chester, she'll ask about the cards the next time she calls. She likes to check up on stuff like that. Last time, she'd seemed disappointed when I said I was saving the journal for something special. She said every day is special. Sooooo obvious she hasn't been to visit in a while!

I thought I could start out with a few of the easy ones, make something of an effort. FRIENDS, EMBARRASSMENT, KISSING, BOYFRIENDS, IDENTITY, SECRETS—there were about a million cards! FRIENDS—how hard could that be?

TEN MINUTES LATER

Okay, not so easy. Do you say, "We're friends because we both hate pink, like black shoes, and talking on the phone"?

It sounds stupid and dumb. Dumb, DUMB, **DUMB**.

It's hard to write something when you know that years later you'll want to read it and have it be cool and interesting, not stupid and lame.

Obviously, I had to give up on a bold and flashy handwriting style because surprisingly, I've got too much to blather on about and it wouldn't all fit on the cards.

FRIENDS

Best Friend—Sandra

She laughs kind of like a baby goat—so even if she is really far away from you, you can tell it's her. This can be either funny or embarrassing, depending on the situation. We've been friends for three years and know almost everything about each other, and except for the fact that she likes to eat "weird meat*" sandwiches, we pretty much like the same things. We are just a perfect friend fit. We can talk on the phone for hours, starting from the minute we get home. Mom says, "What can you possibly have left say? You just saw each other."

It's one of those questions where it doesn't really matter what answer you give because she's really just putting her opinion into a question. I always say something like, "Oh I don't know . . . stuff." It seems to work. Maybe she's just happy I was listening—for once.

*Disturbing meats like tongue and liverwurst . . . but it's not her fault. Her father is from an Eastern European country that no longer exists (I can't remember the name) and has been feeding her the "foods of his youth"—his saying, since she was just a baby, so you can't really blame her for liking them. She developed a taste for disgusting meat products before she knew they were disgusting.

FRIENDS

Becca# —Best Friend Runner-Up

Even though Sandra, Becca, and I are friends, Becca and Sandra hardly ever get together (outside school) without me. I'm like the filling in our friendship sandwich. Becca is the kind of person who always knows exactly what to say— THERMOS it's like having a human safety net to catch all your stupid words before they fall to the floor. Like the time I broke Mr. Bender's thermos.* If someone says, "Hey, my thermos is broken," and you start laughing, it's pretty hard not to seem guilty. Just as Mr. Bender was about to give me the was-it-you? look (teachers are very good at this), Becca started laughing, too. She has one of those contagious laughs—people can't help but join in. Soon at least a dozen people were laughing . . . even Mr. Bender was smiling. "Probably one of my kids," he said, and he put the thermos down on his desk.

   Mr. Bender has two kids—poor kids!

#Every time Becca's parents are around, we have to call her Rebecca because they have a thing about nicknames.
*Michael threw it to me, and instead of just putting it down on the desk I threw it back. So of course he had to show off with a fancy throw that I would never in a million years have caught, so I dropped it.

KISS

First Kiss—Owen (Age 6)

My bedroom—after dark. Mom calls Owen a character.
Dad calls him a kid destined for trouble.* Owen taught me
how to play Truth or Dare. When you're six, the truth part
isn't very exciting so we did more stuff with the dares. For
the kissing dare I had to hold my lips up to his cheek for
what seemed like a boring forever. I guess that's what we
thought kissing was. After a while we decided it would be
more fun to stand in my bedroom window looking out with
our pajama tops off.

*One of the things Dad likes to add an ending exclama-
tion of "Mark my words!" to.

Mom used to get together with Owen's mom, but then they moved away—relief!

I saw a picture of him last year on their Christmas card, and he looked creepy in that you-can't-trust-him way. The kind of guy who would be all octopus hands and want to get his license so he could get a van. He'd probably remember all about that stupid kissing thing we did, and that would be TOOOOO embarrassing!

Second Kiss—Gordon Maynard

It was second grade. I was sitting all by myself and minding my own business when the teacher asked for a volunteer. We all sat at two-person mini-desks. She had her arm around a new kid, Gordon Maynard, probably to keep him from escaping—at the time it seemed friendly enough, but now in hindsight who knows? She said, "Can anyone share a seat with Gordon?" I put my hand up and offered Gordon Maynard half of my desk. I'm sure the teacher said something like, "Thank you Emily for sharing your desk with Gordon. Gordon you may sit next to Emily." Elementary school teachers just love to fill up their sentences with first names. She steered Gordon over to my desk, and he sat down. Of course the whole class had to turn around and watch. How did Strange New Gordon from the front of the class look sitting next to Emily? And then, with everyone watching, he leaned over and kissed my right shoulder. I seriously never wanted to wear that yellow sweater again. Horrible! Horrible! Horrible!

I can't remember much else. Maybe Gordon Maynard moved away. Off to kiss some other poor unsuspecting second grader and ruin her life.

Four cards and I'm already tired of the project! I'm like that — I have a complete deficiency in staying power. I'm a human Post-it. It looks like I'm sticking to something, but really it's sooooo easy to pull me off.

HERE I GO AGAIN

Okay, I decided (personal feel-good goal) if I just do a couple of cards a day, maybe it won't seem like such a take-forever project, and I'll actually be able to finish something. Then I looked through the rest of the cards. I can't believe it! There's only one more Kiss card!

Obviously, I should have used an EMBARRASSMENT card for stupid Gordon Maynard. Now I've gone and wasted a KISS card! Who designed these stupid cards? Like you're supposed to have only three kisses in your entire life? I was going to write about the kiss with XXX—name not revealed to protect the innocent (ME). But now forget it! It doesn't count, anyway. I didn't even tell Sandra about it—so it's almost like it never really happened.

It sounds totally lame and corny but at least one kiss card should be for a real kiss—the kind that comes after days of *kiss-apation* (you know you are going to get kissed, you just don't know where or when it will happen). The kind of kiss you can't wait to tell your friends about, and then do—again and again, until they are so sick of it they tell you to "please shut up about it already!" The kind of kiss you'll want to remember for the rest of your life. The kind of kiss that a girl deserves to have at least once!!!! It's only fair!

KISS ON A PLAQUE
IN MY BRAIN

Chapter 2

TUESDAY

EMBARRASSMENT

Art Class—Everyone

I'M A SIZE...

Pre-embarrassment phase, everything is going well. HA! I had on new jeans and was kind of surprised that people were noticing. Usually, that's not something people pick up on—especially guys. So I'm thinking, "Maybe these jeans make my butt look small. . . . I should have bought more than one pair. . . . I should definitely get another pair over the weekend!" Warning bells go off, and for half a second you feel as if maybe something could be wrong. But what? At that moment, with too many people smiling at me, Mike (good friend that he is) came over and told me that the sticky size sticker was still on my leg. I couldn't believe it! "Why didn't you tell me before?" He said something lame like, "I thought you knew." What's the point of having friends if they are too stupid to help you? Sandra said I shouldn't be so mad at Mike because guys don't have any fashion sense. Well, fashion sense is not a bulletin board advertising your butt size! Sandra said that on an embarrassment scale of one to ten, it was really only a three—four tops. She's big on rating scales. Personally it seemed more like six: three for the event and three for the apology to Mike.* She said she was sure that nobody saw it, but those Gap stickers are long and totally noticeable!

*Nice note dropped in his locker—much easier than having a face-to-face, potentially-even-more-embarrassing apology session.

EMBARRASSMENT

Embarrassment—The Novaks

I have an amazing babysitting job—great money and the kids are usually already asleep. Mrs. Novak likes to put the kids to bed herself. I don't mind just watching TV.

> HELLO MY NAME IS
> KATE

The only bad part of the job is that they think my name is Kate. It all happened so fast. I should have said something that first night when Mr. Novak said, "Thank you, Kate," while handing me my money, but instead I just said, "You're welcome." I think I was too surprised to say anything else. Then Mrs. Novak asked, "Are you available next Friday, Kate?" and after about three or four more rounds of "Kate this" and "Kate that" . . . well, it was too late. I came home and told Mom the whole story. At first she did a lot of head shaking and said she would definitely not cover for me. But when I said she was depriving me of an income, because I would certainly lose my job if they thought their babysitter was some kind of a flake who didn't even know her own name, she changed her mind. She can be kind of cheap. So now they just think Mom's the crazy one. She never remembers I'm supposed to be Kate until partway through the conversation. She'll answer the phone and say something like, "Oh, I'm sorry, you have the wrong number. . . . No wait, damn! Hang on, I'll get her."

Better her than me!

Embarrassment is obviously something I know

a lot about. It took me, like, three seconds to fill out both those cards. Huge example of embarrassment happened today. I was nervous all night about the Sarahs-ignoring-me thing. Should I play it cool like I didn't care that they were ignoring me,

or do what Sandra suggested: "Stand up for yourself and tell them that it was lame and juvenile to ignore you just because you couldn't do what they wanted"? I called Sandra last night to get her opinion on the whole thing. Sometimes I wonder if she's the best person to go to for advice on the Sarahs—she always seems to pick the controversial option. I really hadn't thought the whole thing through enough when I ran into the Sarahs outside my social stud-

FEELING GREAT

RAYS OF
SELF-CONFIDENCE

ies class. They said something about being sorry that I couldn't go with them last night . . . and I said, without even thinking, "Well, maybe I could have if you hadn't ignored me; that was so lame and juvenile!"

Sometimes it feels really great when you stand up for yourself. Unfortunately, it's not so great if you think you are standing up for yourself but you're actually being a weirdo because you misread the entire situation. There was a lot of:

"What do you mean ignoring you?"
"Yesterday, outside school."

"When? We never saw you."

"I was calling you."

"After school?"

"You were walking away from the school and pretending not to hear me."

It was ultra-confusing until we figured out that the Sarahs were not ignoring me but listening to music on Sarah W.'s new MP3 player. That's why they couldn't hear me. It doesn't really matter anyway because now I can tell that Sarah W. is mad that I thought they were ignoring me and that I said they were lame and juvenile—even if it was all a mistake. She wouldn't tell me what the big exciting news was, even though I apologized a bunch of times. Sarah W. said, "It was no big deal; let's just forget it." Great! Of course when you don't know what something is, you always imagine it was amazing and cool. Later, after Sarah W. left, Sarah J. told me it had just been an invitation to have pizza at her house. I told Sandra how I'd missed out on going to Sarah J.'s house, and she said, "It's just like Sarah W. to make a stupid pizza dinner into something big and important!" I didn't say so, but it was kind of big and important. Getting invited over to someone's house is the next step in friendship evolution. I don't think Sandra's ever going to like Sarah W. I should have kept my mouth shut and not told her anything. My friend world is never going to be even close to perfect. And then when I was walking away from Sandra, I smashed my arm against an open locker and yelped. Sandra shook her head in that I-feel-sorry-for-you way that means, "Oh, Emily, you're just such a mess." So here I am, a klutz both socially and physically. Mom says, "You don't pay attention, that's why you're always bumping into things." Maybe, but that hardly explains all the social mistakes. It's like I have my own private mix 'n' match of "saying the wrong thing," "doing the wrong thing," and "not saying anything when you really should say something." SO CONFUSING!!!

MY OWN FLIP BOOK

I used to wonder if maybe I had one of those split personalities, like on TV. Without warning, the split personality (her name is probably something like Jane or Ann—the evil sides of split personalities usually have plain normal names so they don't draw attention to themselves) takes over my body, says or does a couple of stupid things, and then disappears. It would be a nice excuse except that I don't have the memory loss part. You have to have memory loss—like suddenly you find yourself on a stinky bus or in the men's washroom at the mall, and you have no idea how you got there. I can always remember every painful second of the trudge up the hill to the top of Embarrassment Point.

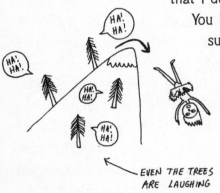

EVEN THE TREES ARE LAUGHING

The only embarrassment-safe people are clowns.

	Clown	Real Person
Can wear red face freely	Yes	No
Can stumble, fall, and wear gobs of mysterious green in teeth	Yes	No
Gets applause for uncoordinated outfits	Yes	No
Is expected to make dumb choices	Yes	No

So how hard can clown school be? Am I a natural? Too bad they're so creepy!

Sandra says it's a self-confidence thing. She said, "Look at the girls at school. Who's got popularity wrapped up with a bow? Kids with older brothers and sisters! It's like they've got the secret guidebook of 'What to Do' and 'What Not to Do.' You, you're out there all alone; no wonder you make a lot of mistakes." Nice way of saying I am a loser?

She seemed especially pleased with her theory. So I said, "Well, what's your excuse?" Nobody likes to be called a loser.

She has an older sister, Claire, who is nice enough but likes country music and endless craft projects—need I say more? Sandra shrugged her shoulders and said, "I was born into the pit of uncool." It's true! Sandra has clawed her way to level ground. She is amazing! There are four geographical formations of sibling coolness:

SIBLING COOLNESS

THE PIT	LEVEL GROUND	SMALL HILL	MOUNTAIN
Older sibling is definitely perceived as odd, strange, or boring.	No older siblings, so you're starting on your own.	Older siblings are well-balanced and generally liked by all.	Older siblings are extra cool or maybe even famous.

I guess I should be thankful. At least I didn't start out in a hole. But what were Mom and Dad doing for those nine kidless years before me? Couldn't they have at least given me a mound to start out on? A sort-of-cute older brother? "Thinking of ourselves and having some fun," says Mom. Thank you, parents!

I've been trying to buy into Sandra's theory, but it seems that almost too much stuff happens to me to blame nonexistent siblings—like that whole Novak babysitting thing. When I first told Sandra about it, she said, "No way" about ten thousand times, which was kind of annoying. Then she said she thought the whole alternative-identity thing was kind of cool—like a spy or a superhero. She said we should create a "Kate personality"—sort of a babysitter extraordinaire. We made a quick list of above-ordinary babysitter attributes—things that parents would find especially comforting when they were leaving their kids for a night out.

ATTRIBUTE	BENEFIT
Wears glasses	Seems trustworthy and not flaky
Calls the kids by their full names—Christopher, instead of Chris	Sounds professional
Has laminated list of emergency phone numbers	Shows commitment to the profession
Always brings homework to do	Looks reliable
Has a chart to check off important information	We didn't design a whole chart but decided it was definitely something that would be impressive

Sandra said the alter ego of Kate (the real-me part) could turn on cable and sample all the treats in the house the moment the parents left. I said I already did that and tried to change the subject when Sandra offered up Claire's skills to sew the letter *K* on a couple of my shirts—"like a uniform/costume thing," she said. "Crafty Fingers is not touching my clothes!" I said. "Well, it wouldn't be tacky!" said Sandra. "Claire can do lots of fancy stitches like embroidery and cross-hatching!" Sometimes it's hard to remember the Friend Sister Rule since it's kind of a tricky one.

FRIEND SISTER RULE

If you have a sister, you can make fun of her and call her names anytime you want. If your best friend has a sister, you should only make fun of the sister, or call the sister names if your best friend has already done so in the last 30 seconds.

I tried to say something nice about Claire so Sandra would know I was sorry about calling her Crafty Fingers. "Yeah, well, she's probably too busy anyway," said Sandra, and I knew that everything was okay again.

I was thinking about filling out another card, but I could hear Mom banging away in the kitchen. She was doing her unhappy-baker routine! It's really distracting! If she's going to make all that noise grumbling with the cookware, Dad should be the one who has to listen to it, not me! I don't even think he was home. Sometimes I just wish they'd get divorced like normal parents.

PARENTS' RELATIONSHIP PATTERN

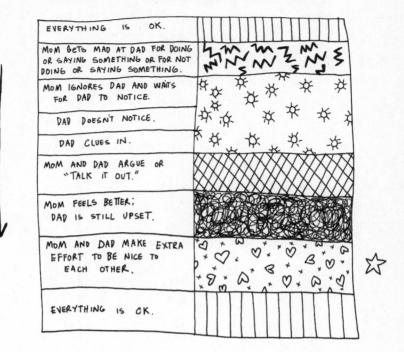

EVERYTHING IS OK.	
MOM GETS MAD AT DAD FOR DOING OR SAYING SOMETHING OR FOR NOT DOING OR SAYING SOMETHING.	
MOM IGNORES DAD AND WAITS FOR DAD TO NOTICE.	
DAD DOESN'T NOTICE.	
DAD CLUES IN.	
MOM AND DAD ARGUE OR "TALK IT OUT."	
MOM FEELS BETTER; DAD IS STILL UPSET.	
MOM AND DAD MAKE EXTRA EFFORT TO BE NICE TO EACH OTHER.	
EVERYTHING IS OK.	

READ DOWN

☆ Even though this is a make-up phase, it is kind of sickening to watch. There's lots of touching and not-so-secret smiles.

I once made a list of a few of the things they could improve upon but chickened out about giving it to them. It's like that movie perspective that Aunt Chester talks about. It's easier to see what's going on when you are on the outside.

Enough about them . . . back to me!

ME! ME! ME!

SANDRA USED TO CALL ME "EM,"
WHICH IS "ME" SPELLED BACKWARDS.

Chapter 3

WEDNESDAY

Map Of Me

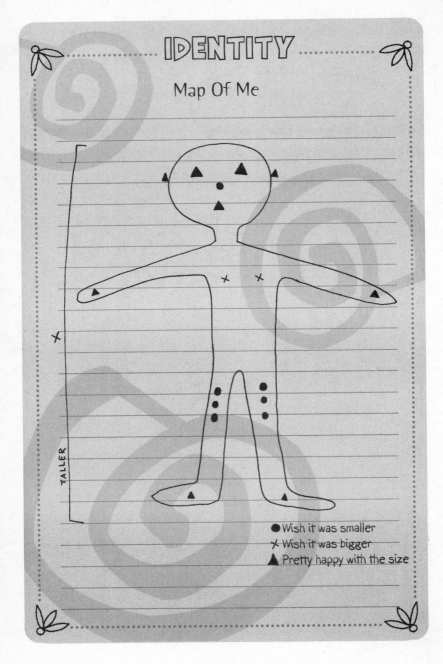

TALLER

● Wish it was smaller
✗ Wish it was bigger
▲ Pretty happy with the size

it's pretty hard to reinvent yourself. People get freaked out if you try. There was this girl at school last year. Her name was Dusty, kind of a horse name. She came back to school after a long weekend and said that she'd changed her name to Renee. She didn't seem any different except for the name. People just didn't want to call her Renee—it seemed stupid. Besides, we all knew her real name was Dusty. It was like calling a couch a sofa—nicer name but same chair. She left class in the middle of the year—probably moved to a new school where they didn't know anything about Dusty and thought she looked and sounded just like a Renee.

A SMARTER, WISER EMILY

CAN THINK OF WITTY COMEBACKS IN TIME TO USE THEM

ABLE TO CONTROL BLUSHING AT WILL

KNOWS WHEN NOT TO SAY ANYTHING

CAN PROPERLY EVALUATE A SITUATION IN JUST SECONDS

ALWAYS HAS THE RIGHT ANSWER

A smarter, wiser me would know what to do next about the Sarahs thing. Considering how it turned out yesterday, I should probably do nothing—and not breathe a word of it to Sandra, the controversy queen. Pretend nothing happened.

After I'd been home from school for about twenty minutes, Mom knocked on my door and gave me the I-haven't-heard-you-practice-the-clarinet-yet-today speech. It used to be a lot longer and included variations on the themes of "If you aren't going to practice, we'll just take it back," "It's not my job to be after you all day to practice," and "I guess your father was right after all." Dad said my interest in the clarinet would only last as long as a sandwich at a picnic. What does that mean? He has this way of saying stupid things with lots of conviction so that sometimes they almost seem to make sense. She's so bossy when Dad is not around for her to ignore. Next she'll be organizing some kind of emergency cleaning chore. I wish she were more like Sandra's mom. Whenever she's mad at Sandra's dad she goes shopping. Sandra has a lot of nice outfits; we just have a sporadically tidy house. I yelled at Mom that I was studying, but I don't think she cared. She just wanted to deliver her nagging message. Feel better, Mom? She loves to try and make me feel guilty about the clarinet.

I usually try to practice at least three times a week, but it's hard. Okay, who am I kidding? Two times a week . . . maybe. The clarinet is not an instrument that sounds that great when you are playing by yourself, especially if you are third clarinet. It's really the lamest of all the clarinet positions. First clarinet gets to play solos and usually lots of the melody. Second clarinet supports first clarinet but still gets to play some of the melody. Third clarinet is completely boring and hardly ever gets to play any fun stuff—just lots of long background notes. It's easy, but not much fun. The only good part about playing the clarinet is the other people in the band. Sandra plays the trumpet, which is not really a girl-type instrument, but she pulls it off. Becca plays the bassoon—

a long black instrument that sounds like a dying goose (seriously). It also rhymes with baboon, which is unfortunate if people are going to pick on you. As far as any of us can tell, Becca is not very talented, but maybe the bassoon is just really hard to play. Becca is really athletic and on all sorts of sports teams. It's kind of funny that we're friends since I'm such a klutz. We don't do stuff together every day like I do with Sandra, but we usually hang out a couple of times a week. You don't have to see someone every day to be great friends with them. I think Becca feels that sometimes Sandra and I are too silly for her because she once said, "A little of you two can go a long way." It's not that she's serious and doesn't have a sense of humor—she does—but she's just not super girlish, not the type of girl who does a lot of giggling.

Then there are the two Sarahs. Sarah J. plays the clarinet and Sarah W. plays the flute. Why do all the cute girls play the flute? Sarah W. is the kind of girl that all the guys love. You stand next to her (she's small and perfect) and feel like a thumb. She's best friends with Sarah J., which can sometimes be confusing. Like the time she said, "Sarah has a crush on David," because at first I thought she was talking about herself in that annoying third-person way that some people do. But then I realized she was talking about Sarah J., because there is no way Sarah W. would like someone like David. Sometimes we eat lunch together, but I have never been to their houses and, until Monday, never almost-been invited to do anything with them outside of school. The Sarahs are pretty popular and can hang out with the cool kids and then the not-so-cool kids like me. I don't know how they do it, but everybody seems to like them. Sandra says I could probably be better friends with the Sarahs if I weren't friends with her. I told her she was wrong, but I'm not sure the Sarahs are that crazy about her. Good thing I don't have to choose. (Of course I would totally pick Sandra.)

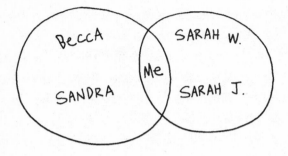

Sandra says guys like Sarah W. because she has nice boobs (like Sandra is suddenly some kind of boob expert?), is not so smart, and knows how to flirt. I think it's more complicated than that, but I didn't say anything because it sounded like Sandra was jealous, and if someone is jealous, there isn't anything you can say that will change her mind. Too bad!

It's hard not to be envious of someone who has everything. Sarah W. is definitely one of those someones, but she's not a big show-off. She's fun to hang out with and kind of makes you feel important just by being with her. Plus she's pretty funny—in a goofy/ditzy sort of way. It's almost like she's always a little surprised that people seem to like her so much (unless it's a guy). She definitely knows that guys like her.

Everyone likes Sarah J. She plays the second clarinet and sits three seats to the left of me—she's a much better player than I am. She and Sarah W. have been friends forever. Their moms met in a prenatal (pre-baby) exercise class and got to be friends. I guess they're almost like sisters, except no one would give sisters the same name. I couldn't believe that she had a crush on David. I suppose he's nice enough, but he always says weird things when you talk to him. Sandra says it's because he's nervous around girls. Sarah J. says she doesn't care because she thinks he's funny—in a comic genius way, not in a clown way. The last time I saw him, I asked him a question about English class. Instead of answering my question he said, "What kind of noodle would you be if you had to be a noodle? You know, lasagna noodle, fettuccine, or linguine?" I couldn't think of what to say, so I told him I'd have to think about it. The annoying thing about David is that he believes everything you say. So when I gave him the "I'll think about it" brush-off, he really was expecting an answer. Every time I saw him in class or in the hall, he'd give me a "Well, what's your answer?" look. Finally I just said, "Penne." Penne—a versatile everyday kind of noodle. Nothing too fancy or fussy.

PeNNe NooDle

I asked Sarah J. what kind of noodle she had picked for David's noodle thing. She looked at me like I was crazy. It's obviously not a very big census if I'm the only person he asked. I'm a weirdo magnet!

Sandra said Sarah J. would probably be spaghetti, because everybody likes spaghetti. Then she started talking about Sarah W., and I could tell she was trying to think of something mean to say, so I changed the subject. Keeping four friends happy at once is hard. There are just too many opportunities for somebody to be upset about something. It would obviously be easier if we were all one big, happy gang. But I don't do so well in big groups. I'm more of a friend-here, friend-there kind of person—more buffet style.

It's too bad because it really makes things more complicated. Like the time I forgot my coat at Sandra's house, and she wore it without asking me. She (big surprise) ran into Sarah W. at the park, and Sarah W. said, "Hey, Emily has a coat like that."

"No, she doesn't," said Sandra. And she walked off hoping that Sarah W. would just forget about the whole thing, which was really stupid because girls always notice things like clothes and nobody forgets an act of obnoxious rudeness. Of course I heard all about it the next day. I wasn't so mad about the coat, but it took forever to get Sandra and Sarah W. back to a sort of friendly status.

"A number nine on the stupid scale," admitted Sandra.

Friends are tricky that way.

There are lots of levels of friendshipness. Sometimes it's not so easy to know where to put a friend.

FRIENDSHIP CATEGORIES

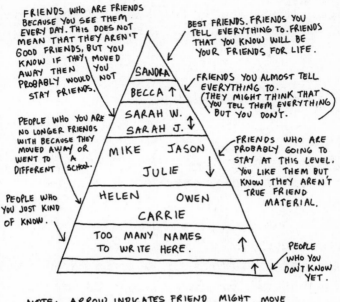

FRIENDS WHO ARE FRIENDS BECAUSE YOU SEE THEM EVERY DAY. THIS DOES NOT MEAN THAT THEY AREN'T GOOD FRIENDS, BUT YOU KNOW IF THEY MOVED AWAY THEN YOU PROBABLY WOULD NOT STAY FRIENDS.

BEST FRIENDS. FRIENDS YOU TELL EVERYTHING TO. FRIENDS THAT YOU KNOW WILL BE YOUR FRIENDS FOR LIFE.

FRIENDS YOU ALMOST TELL EVERYTHING TO. (THEY MIGHT THINK THAT YOU TELL THEM EVERYTHING BUT YOU DON'T.)

PEOPLE WHO YOU ARE NO LONGER FRIENDS WITH BECAUSE THEY MOVED AWAY OR WENT TO A DIFFERENT SCHOOL.

FRIENDS WHO ARE PROBABLY GOING TO STAY AT THIS LEVEL. YOU LIKE THEM BUT KNOW THEY AREN'T TRUE FRIEND MATERIAL.

PEOPLE WHO YOU JUST KIND OF KNOW.

PEOPLE WHO YOU DON'T KNOW YET.

SANDRA
BECCA ↑
SARAH W.
SARAH J. ↕
MIKE   JASON ↓
JULIE
HELEN   OWEN
CARRIE
TOO MANY NAMES TO WRITE HERE.

NOTE: ARROW INDICATES FRIEND MIGHT MOVE UP OR DOWN TO A NEW LEVEL.

Carrie

When I was six, Carrie moved onto my street, three houses away. We saw each other every day after school and all day on the weekends.

As soon as she started high school (she was two years older than me), she didn't want to be friends anymore. I guess she was too old for me. High-school girls don't hang out with grade-school girls. She still lives down the street. Sometimes when I see her it's a little weird. We both just say hi and keep walking. We kind of pretend that we never really knew each other.

THE LOOK-RIGHT-PAST-YOU LOOK

We've pretty much perfected this look.

Helen
We used to be friends in grade school but now never see each other except in the grocery store. (She works there on Saturdays.)

Julie
Julie is one of Mom's friends' kids. When we were little, we did a lot of stuff together. We hardly see each other anymore, but we hear about each other all the time. Mom is always giving me updates on what Julie is doing. When we do see each other, it's kind of uncomfortable because we both know all sorts of things about each other but haven't spent any time together. It kind of leaves us with nothing to talk about. I keep telling Mom not to tell Julie's mom every little thing I do. It's like almost being a celebrity—but in a boring, you-know-you're-nothing-special way. Parents don't seem to understand that their friends' kids aren't always going to be perfect friend matches. Not that Julie isn't nice; she is, but we don't really have a whole lot in common. If she went to my school, I'm sure she'd be one of the cool girls who hangs out by the fence during lunch and break. I try to fake

hipness when we have to get together, but she always talks about music and stuff that I've never heard of before. It's probably annoying for her.

I've got a questionnaire that kind of clears up that gray area between true friend and just friend-friend. If I answer yes to at least five of the questions on the chart, then that person is a true friend.

FRIEND QUESTIONNAIRE

Questions	Yes	No
Would I trust them with a secret?		
Would I completely die if they saw me dancing in my underpants?		
Would I invite them over and risk their being horrified by my parents?		
Would I show them the trick of how when I cross my eyes I can let my left eye move away from my nose while my right eye stays crossed?		
Would I admit to liking beets and tell them the beet story?		
Would I not hide the too-cutesy stuffed animals grandma gave me, before showing off my room?		
Would I be more grateful than embarrassed if they told me I had something weird in my teeth?		
Would I make jokes and not feel stupid?		

BEET STORY

The day after you eat beets you will think you are going to die—especially if you eat a lot of beets. Beets should have a warning label!

WARNING
- CONSUMPTION OF TOO MANY BEETS WILL LEAD TO WEIRD SIDE EFFECTS.
- STAY CALM... YOUR POOP WILL BE RED.
- YOU WILL NOT DIE.
- DO NOT TELL EVERYONE YOU KNOW THAT YOU ARE GOING TO DIE.
- DO NOT CALL YOUR DOCTOR.
- IT WILL GO AWAY.

To date, the most embarrassing story of my life . . . I could hear the nurse telling a doctor about it in the other room and laughing as we (Mom and I) left the emergency room. Some things are so embarrassing that your face gets red when you think about them.

Finally! Dad came home. He was asking Mom the same question—"What's for dinner, Adna?"—over and over and louder and louder. It always takes him about six or seven tries until he clues in that something is wrong, and no, Mom has not developed some kind of freaky hearing problem. She's just ignoring him. The whole thing is annoyingly childish.

We had a completely uncomfortable forty-five minutes at the dinner table, and on top of that, we had a rip-off dessert. Grapes are not dessert! Mom said she tried to bake a tart but burned the crust because she was thinking about something else . . . and then she gave Dad one of her you-are-so-guilty looks. Dad made a big show of saying how juicy and tasty the grapes were. If you give someone real dessert (pies, cakes, tarts, pudding, etc.) after dinner for every day of their life, you can't just take it away. It's punishment! I'm going to have to go and eat a spoonful of sugar!

SPOON OF SUGAR

Chapter 4

THURSDAY

FRIENDS

WHO ARE BOYS

Mike

Mike has his locker next to mine. When you see some-one twenty times a day, there is a high chance you will be friends. Mike is funny (Ha! Ha! funny, not weird funny). He also writes really good notes—the kind you get in your locker for fun, not the kind you take in class.

Jason

Jason lives next door. He is almost exactly the same age as I am (I'm fourteen days older), but he goes to a different school. We've known each other forever. He's kind of like a cousin—not as close as a brother, but someone who knows more about me than any other guy. Sandra has a pre-crush on Jason. She doesn't like to make a full-crush commitment until she knows that the guy likes her back. So far we can't tell if Jason likes her or not. Sandra says if he were her boyfriend, she'd borrow his burgundy sweater and brown jacket and never give them back.

   She's right!

   His brown jacket is really nice.

YOU might think that a boy is just your friend, but then if you find out that maybe he likes you (in a boyfriend way), everything changes instantly.

Now you've got the mess of figuring out which path to take.

FRIEND OR BOYFRIEND?

ACKNOWLEDGE · NO

DENIAL

EVADE

ACKNOWLEDGE · YES

THIS IS LIKE THE ≈♡≈ JACKPOT!

YOU WILL BE HAPPY, YOU WILL WISH EVERYONE COULD BE AS HAPPY AS YOU, THEY WILL WISH SO TOO.

IF YOU DON'T LIKE HIM BACK IN THAT BOYFRIEND WAY, START TALKING A LOT ABOUT HOW BOYFRIENDS ARE ENTIRELY OVERRATED AND TOO MUCH TROUBLE, BUT BE CAREFUL BECAUSE SOME PEOPLE (LIKE SANORA) WILL SAY THEY ABSOLUTELY DO NOT LIKE SO-AND-SO...BUT WHEN THEY FIND OUT THAT SO-AND-SO LIKES THEM, THEY SLOWLY CHANGE THEIR MINDS AND END UP BEING IN ♡ WITH SO-AND-SO.

PRETEND YOU DON'T KNOW THAT HE LIKES YOU AND HOPE THAT HE NEVER BRINGS IT UP, BECAUSE YOU JUST WANT TO BE FRIENDS.

TELL HIM YOU DON'T LIKE HIM BACK AND HOPE YOU CAN STILL BE GOOD FRIENDS. GOOD LUCK.

NOTE: BOYS ARE MOST OFTEN VERY SNEAKY ABOUT LETTING YOU KNOW THEY LIKE YOU.

In theory, the boyfriend thing seems pretty great. I mean, who wouldn't want a guy to really like them? You'd do things together every day and finally have someone to hug whenever you want. Little kids get hugs all the time, but somewhere along the growing-up line they stop happening. And then there you are, hugless except on birthdays and special holidays (and not always wanting to be hugged by some distant relative who maybe forgot their deodorant that day). No one to hold except an old stuffed animal. That's why some girls are really into the horse thing—something big and soft to cuddle up to. Really, it's only the everyday part of having a boyfriend that worries me—I'm fine with the fantasy part. How does real-life Boyfriend World fit together? What happens to my friends? Is my best friend still my best friend, or is my boyfriend now my best friend? Then there are my parents. Would they be happy for me or be complete overreacting freaks? Plus, there's everyone at school. It almost ruins it—almost but not quite. I still want one!

Sandra said Andrew Wright was staring at me today. I said, "No way!" Andrew Wright would never be interested in me, not in a million years. He hangs out with the cool kids—though he seems a lot friendlier.

She said, "No, I saw it with my own eyes—he was looking right at you." Sandra can be so stubborn when she's got something in her head.

I tried anyway: "Sandra! Come off it! I probably had something weird stuck in my hair or my teeth. There's not a chance in the world that Andrew would be looking at me."

"Was too."

"Was not."

"Was too!"

"Was not!"

I could tell she was going to go on and on about it, so I broke down and told her about the card project to get her off the subject. She says she can't believe I have the energy to fill out all the cards—she knows about my failed four-sentence journal effort. I told her that somehow this one seemed easier, maybe because it wasn't just a bunch of blank pages. Then she said, "Can I see them? When you're all done? It'll be like a test. You can quiz me, on you . . . with the flashcards." I just knew she'd ask to see them—which is why I wasn't going to tell her anything about it. I don't think I could write down everything if I knew someone else was going to read them—even when the someone is Sandra. If life were like the movies, I'd have two sets of cards: a fake set to show around and then the real set for me (they always do that in Dad's gangster movies). I ended up telling Sandra she could see them, but it was one of those temporary lies—until I could think of how to keep them from her or until she forgot about them. (Highly unlikely.)

About an hour after dinner, Mom knocked on my door to ask me if I wanted a donut. Dad always comes home with a box of them after he and Mom have been fighting. It's like his peace offering—no wonder Mom can't lose any weight!

We just ate dinner with dessert (walnut cake).

How could I be hungry? She wants me to eat them so she won't. She can't stand to see lonely donuts in a box.

So now their fight is over. I don't even know what this one was about.

Sometimes it's so obvious that Mom just needs more attention—maybe more friends or something. It's really too bad that Aunt Chester lives so far away.

Chapter 5

FRIDAY

HATE

Things I Hate

When something is broken and no matter how hard you try to fix it, you know it is going to stay broken.

- David—I'm never going to even look at him again!
- Stickers—Who invented sticker glue? It's like cement! I've been picking at the sticker of the kittens playing ping-pong for years! I still can't get it off.*
- Clowns.
- Not having my own computer.**
- Penne noodles.

*One of the hundred stupid stickers I put everywhere in my room when I was eight. It's on the side of my night table. I only notice it when I'm lying down and too sleepy to do anything about it. It's always the last thing I see before I turn out the light.

**I have to share one with "the family."

Dad set up a computer room in the basement, which is dark, smelly (Dad says, "It's your imagination. I don't smell anything."), and probably party central for mice and spiders as soon as the lights go out. I don't go down there much, which is causing some problems.

START

I DON'T GO DOWN TO THE DUNGEON ROOM BECAUSE IT'S CREEPY

DAD SAYS, "DON'T BE A CHILD."

DAD SAYS, "YOU HARDLY USE THE COMPUTER—WHY SHOULD WE HAVE IT TAKING UP SPACE UPSTAIRS?"

I SAY, "I'D USE IT MORE IF IT WASN'T IN THE CELLAR."

i can't believe it. Now Sarah J. is mad at me! It's one of those things where you could spend hours thinking, Is she mad at me? Is she not mad at me? Then finally you find out.

She is definitely mad! And not mad because of the "lame and juvenile" thing. No! This is a brand new mad! A surprise mad— because it totally came out of nowhere! Here are some clues so that you will know if someone is mad at you. Because very often people will not tell you they are mad . . . they want you to be psychic and guess.

ARE THEY MAD?

	MAD
THEY ANSWER ANY QUESTION YOU ASK THEM WITH A ONE-WORD ANSWER.	X
THEY DON'T LOOK AT YOUR FACE WHEN YOU ARE TALKING.	X
THEY PRETEND THEY CAN'T HEAR YOU.	X
THEY PRETEND THEY CAN'T SEE YOU.	X
IF YOUR NAME IS MENTIONED, THEY ROLL THEIR EYES.	X
THEY DO LOTS OF HEAVY SIGHING IF YOU ARE TALKING TO SOMEONE NEAR THEM.	X

Unfortunately, this is just level one of "mad at you," and there are at least three other levels. It's important to deal with the problem before it gets to level two, which is much worse and can often include nasty words, rumors, and maybe even backstabbing.

Sarah thinks I like David, or more horrifying—David likes me!

It's all because of his stupid noodle survey. All week long she's been waiting for him to ask what kind of noodle she'd like to be, but he never asked her. She picked capellini because she said it was innocent yet sort of sexy. Whatever! I can't believe this! I truly, truly, truly do not in any way, even if he was the last guy on earth, like David!!

It's not like I can say, "Sarah, I don't like David. In fact I think he's a bit of a weirdo." It would be like saying, "Sarah, you have awful taste and you're a weirdo for liking him." It's hard to get people to believe you when they already have a thought in their head that they believe to be true—even if they are wrong. Just saying, "No, you are wrong" hardly ever works. There is a sacred rule among girlfriends.

GIRLFRIEND SACRED RULE

Friends can never "like" the same guy unless he is a celebrity or totally unattainable.

Unattainable meaning an older guy—like way older (five years plus), and maybe he works in the bookstore or copy shop or the restaurant. Someone you could just sort of safely flirt with. . . . Maybe!

GIRLFRIEND SUB-SACRED RULE

Once a friend has "claimed a crush" (said she likes a guy), that guy is off-limits no matter how much you may also secretly like him.

I can't believe that Sarah thinks I'm such a bad friend. That she thinks I would break the rule! Now would be a good time to turn into an ostrich.

Decided to call Sandra and complain.

LATER

Sandra was no help. She said, "Anyone who thinks you like David is an idiot." She's right. This whole mix-up is stupid. I'm never going to eat penne noodles again. We talked for only twenty minutes because Sandra said she definitely had to go that second. Claire was standing in the doorway giving her the evil eye.

I don't think she'd be too upset if I never spoke to the Sarahs again. Of course, I don't just have one Sarah mad at me—the Sarahs always come as a double pack.

Must think nice, positive thoughts!

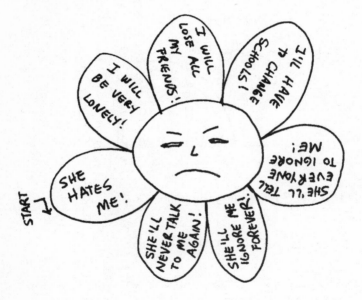

Things always look worse at night, when it's dark. Tomorrow everything will be . . . less bad.

Chapter 6

SUNDAY

REGRETS

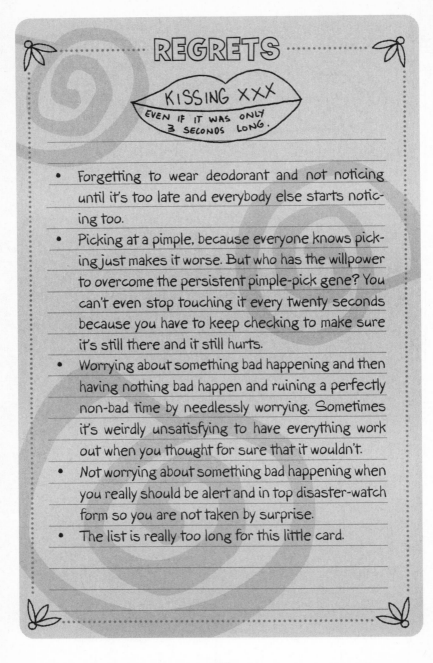

KISSING XXX

EVEN IF IT WAS ONLY 3 SECONDS LONG.

- Forgetting to wear deodorant and not noticing until it's too late and everybody else starts noticing too.
- Picking at a pimple, because everyone knows picking just makes it worse. But who has the willpower to overcome the persistent pimple-pick gene? You can't even stop touching it every twenty seconds because you have to keep checking to make sure it's still there and it still hurts.
- Worrying about something bad happening and then having nothing bad happen and ruining a perfectly non-bad time by needlessly worrying. Sometimes it's weirdly unsatisfying to have everything work out when you thought for sure that it wouldn't.
- Not worrying about something bad happening when you really should be alert and in top disaster-watch form so you are not taken by surprise.
- The list is really too long for this little card.

Chapter 7

MONDAY

CLOTHES
What I Know

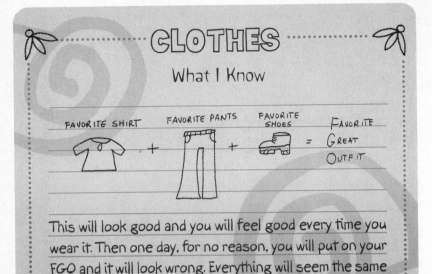

FAVORITE SHIRT + FAVORITE PANTS + FAVORITE SHOES = FAVORITE GREAT OUTFIT

This will look good and you will feel good every time you wear it. Then one day, for no reason, you will put on your FGO and it will look wrong. Everything will seem the same but it won't be. The FGO time limit will have run out.

It's okay to check yourself out in the reflection of a store window if you pretend to be looking at the window display.

If you start to notice that every time you wear a certain shirt, sweater, or dress, something bad happens—that shirt, sweater, or dress could be a piece of BKC (Bad Karma Clothing). Not everyone believes in this—Sandra says it's stupid, but the Sarahs both have clothes (a coat and a T-shirt) that they no longer wear because of it. So far I haven't noticed anything particularily suspicious about any of my outfits. The bad luck seems to be spread around pretty evenly.

i just knew today was going to be horrible, even though I tried hard and wore my second favorite shirt, my first favorite being dirty since I wore it on Saturday to try and make myself feel better—it didn't do much good, but I suppose I looked nice. Then, on top of everything else, I had a full-grown pimple on my chin! How come a pimple that is this big O on paper looks about as big as an eyeball when it's on your face? I asked Sandra if it was completely noticeable, and she said no and that she thought it was a crumb of toast or something left over from breakfast. The light in my bathroom sucks! I obviously used the wrong color skin-tone cover stick. I had to spend the whole morning thinking of ways to hold my hand, pen, or book casually up in front of my chin to cover it up—sort of a deep-thought look. I don't think it was very successful because Mike kept asking me what was wrong. Finally I told him I had a lot of personal things to think about. He seemed offended, like he wanted me to confide in him or something.

Sandra said she saw him later in class, and he asked her if I was mad at him. Sure! I'm acting all weird because of him! I just can't figure out how to deal with him anymore. At lunchtime Sandra ran across the street to the store and got me a better cover stick. She's the best! She said, "It looks great. For sure no one will be able to see it anymore." It was nice of her, but you can tell when people are looking at your chin—I was glad to get out of there and come home.

EYES LOOKING AT CHIN

I walk in the door and what does Mom say? "Oh, Emily, you've got a pimple on your chin," and then she points like she's being helpful. Like I hadn't noticed! Like the world hadn't noticed!! I ran upstairs and built an Everest-sized mountain

of cream on my chin. It's amazing how something so small can ruin your day! I didn't even see the Sarahs. They were probably avoiding me.

Chapter 8

TUESDAY

SURPRISE

I've secretly always wanted a surprise birthday party. A party filled with friends (actually more than four people), great food, and invisible parents (I suppose they would have to be there since they would pay for it) who are wonderful and just stand in the background and do ABSOLUTELY NOTHING to embarrass me. Everyone would have an amazing time, and I'd get loads of perfect surprise presents—things I hadn't asked for but that I truly love and don't have to pretend to like just to be nice and not hurt anyone's feelings. Basically, it's the kind of thing you see on TV or hear about other people having. I tell everyone that I hate surprise parties—it's safer that way. Usually I just set something up with Sandra and Becca. It's no surprise, but it's fun!

Generally, good surprises are just called "surprises." (I'd like a lot more of these.)

Bad surprises are called "disasters."

(I know all about these!)

HAPPY BIRTHDAY

SANDRA

REBECCA

SURPRISES CAN MORPH INTO DISASTERS WITHOUT WARNING.

Sandra solved my problem without my even knowing about it —which is kind of the bad part. Before class this morning, Sarah J. came up to me from behind and put her arm around my shoulders.

At first I thought, Oh my god. Maybe she's going to choke me, or worse, maybe she wants to wrestle. I can't wrestle—I'm wearing a skirt! That was really stupid because:

1.   When in my life have I ever seen Sarah J. wrestle anybody?
2.   I wouldn't know how to wrestle no matter what I was wearing.

Sometimes my imagination just goes crazy.

Sarah gave me a big shoulder hug and said she was sorry. I was so shocked! I just mumbled something like, "Oh . . . sure . . . okay." I didn't start thinking about it until about five minutes later in French class. Why did she change her mind? Why was she no longer mad?

Sandra kept catching my eye from the other side of the class and giving me the thumbs-up sign. I like French class, except that Mademoiselle Swanson made us all pick French names (mine's Lisette—the only thing I could think of under pressure) and then sit in alphabetical order. So Sandra is sitting off with the Ys (Yvonne). Stupidly, I thought Sandra was just really excited about our assignment. Write a one-page comic in French. (Sandra likes to draw and is really good at it.)

This is a good example of yet another one of my problems— the there's-too-much-stuff-going-on-at-the-same-time problem. Sometimes it's hard to decipher what's really happening.

What my life is like.

What I wish my life was like.

After class, Sandra came running over to me and said, "Isn't it great?"

"Sure," I answered. "What do you want to write about?"

"No!" said Sandra. "The Sarah thing. Didn't you see her? She's looking for you. It's all worked out. She believes you! She's going to apologize. I told her everything!" In

general, an "I told her everything" is something you should be wary of. When she's excited Sandra gives out lots of information at once. It took a while, but Sandra finally told me the whole story. In a nutshell (literally), this is it.

SHE TOLD SARAH J. THAT I HAD A CRUSH ON ANDREW WRIGHT!

And then the conversation went something like this:

ME: You what?

SANDRA: It was the only way.

ME: What?

SANDRA: She'd only believe you didn't like David if I said you liked someone else.

ME: But I don't like Andrew!

SANDRA: Why not? He likes you.

ME: He does not!

SANDRA: He's always looking at you.

ME: Once because I had something in my teeth!

SANDRA: No! He likes you.

ME: Does not!

SANDRA: Does so!

ME: Does not!

SANDRA: Does so.

ME: Shut up!

(ABOUT 54 SECONDS OF SILENCE)

ME: What if she tells him?

SANDRA: She won't.

ME: She could say something by accident.

SANDRA: She wouldn't. She's your friend.

ME: Well I don't really like him.

SANDRA: How about shoes?

ME: What?

SANDRA: For the comic!

Even though friends say they are interested in your life, they never really want to talk about you as much as you want them to. I could have probably talked about the Andrew issue 40% more, just to get it cleared up. Anyway, so now Sandra and I are doing a comic about shoes, Sarah is my friend again and everything is almost all right—except for that Andrew crush thing—which is not really a thing. It's no thing.

LATER

Just smashed my arm on the side of my dresser. It's like my arms and legs are too long for my body. Or my brain can't remember where they are, so they just swing around constantly bumping into things.

I'll soon have a huge bruise tattoo the size of a small eggplant. Mom always gets upset in that shake-her-head, heavy-sigh way every time I have a new bruise or scrape. It's like she thinks I'm a klutz on purpose to punish her or something. It's going to look fantastic with the short-sleeved shirt I am going to wear tomorrow!

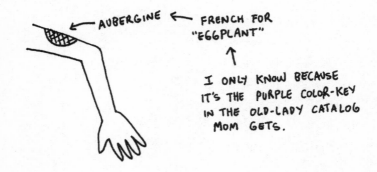

AUBERGINE ← FRENCH FOR "EGGPLANT"

I ONLY KNOW BECAUSE IT'S THE PURPLE COLOR-KEY IN THE OLD-LADY CATALOG MOM GETS.

Chapter 9

WeDNesDAY

REGRETS

Are Complicated

Nobody knows the absolute truth about anybody else. Everybody keeps secrets. It just seems that the closer you are to someone maybe the fewer secrets you have from them. But then if you are really close to someone (your best friend, your boyfriend, husband), you're not really supposed to have any secrets at all. So when they find out you had a secret it's more hurtful because they thought you were 100% truthful with them.

For example:

Not telling Sarah J. about XXX = 20% hurtful

Not telling Becca about XXX = 40% hurtful

Not telling Sandra about XXX = 85% hurtful

Secret Keepers

There are some people who definitely can't keep secrets. Telling one of these people a secret is like saying, "Here, make a flyer and give it to everyone you know."

The Sarahs are being especially nice to me. It's like I've had an instant power-up of charm, and they just can't get enough. All because they think I like Andrew—surprising—even having a pretend crush on someone popular can make you cooler? Sandra and Becca came over after school and we stood outside on the front lawn, in the freezing cold, for about half an hour. Sandra wanted to see if Jason would come out. She was hoping he would be wearing his brown jacket so that she could point it out to Becca. It was a little like shopping at an expensive store (you look and wish but you can't really buy) since:

1. We don't know if Jason likes Sandra.
2. If he does, is it really all that easy to borrow a jacket and never give it back?

Jason never came out. I'm not really good-enough friends with him to call him on the phone. Besides, maybe he wasn't even home. Sandra didn't seem very upset and actually said, "Oh well, there are other fish in the sea," which of course I jumped all over.

"Which fish? Where? When?" But she wouldn't give out any information.

Becca was no help either. She said, "Oh, let's talk about tampons and boobs." Becca is convinced that guys think that when girls get together all they want to talk about are their periods and boobs. It's kind of become her joke way of changing the subject.

We ate about a hundred chocolate-chip-and-walnut cookies and talked about nothing important. I wish Mom would show some self-control. I'm getting pretty tired of nut-infested everything! It's not like you can pick them out either. They are practically ground to a pulp so there is no way she'd ever be able to eat around them. Sandra kept looking at me in that I've-got-a-secret way. Every time I gave her the well-tell-me-then look, she'd just put on her pretend confused face and say, "What?"

Becca finally said, "Well, I've had enough cookies and fun. I'm leaving so you two can stop with the eye games."

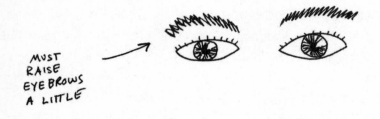

MUST
RAISE
EYE BROWS
A LITTLE

INTENSE LOOK MEANING "TELL ME"

Becca is so together, she wasn't even jealous that maybe there was a secret she wouldn't be part of. I though for sure Sandra would stay and tell me who she liked, but she said, "Yeah, I've got to go too." And they both left together!

My head was just reeling with questions. Did she tell Becca? Why would she tell Becca and not me? Does she suspect about the XXX kiss? Is she punishing me because she thinks I have a secret **from her?** How would she even know that? She's not the least bit psychic—but what if XXX told her! No. Sandra's not that sneaky—I'd totally be able to tell if she knew something. Sometimes you just don't realize how you'll react to something until you are actually faced with it. Like not telling Sandra about XXX—it's not that hard to keep it from her, and before it happened I thought that I would always tell her pretty much everything.

The whole secret thing is hard to get a handle on . . . who knows, who doesn't know, who suspects, and even who knows because they heard by accident—like the time Mom went and had coffee with an old boyfriend from college but didn't tell Dad. She told Aunt Chester it would have been too complicated, besides "Daryl" had a real case of the loss and growths (hair and stomach). So if he had looked amazing she would have told Dad?

After I heard it, I started keeping tabs on her for a couple of weeks for signs of suspicious behavior. In movies the cheating spouse is always extra friendly to their husband/wife to put them off the trail. Mostly she seemed fine, though she did buy Dad some new underwear (the white brief kind, not cool boxers)—hardly wanted to explore that too closely! Finally I just got bored and decided everything was probably okay. She has a pretty dull life—maybe she could use some excitement. I wonder if Daryl is rich and generous with presents.

LATER

I phoned Sandra—couldn't help myself. It was a need-to-know crisis. She was all chatty about everything except her "fish in the sea" comment. Finally I said, "What's that fish thing you mentioned? Who's the fish? Why won't you tell me?"

"Because," she said, "from one to ten it's only a two. When it's a five I'll tell you." I couldn't believe it. Like that was supposed to satisfy me. That's basically saying, "I HAVE A SECRET AND I'M NOT GOING TO TELL YOU!"

I tried again. "Come on, that's not fair. I tell you everything! We're best friends! You're supposed to tell me stuff!" She was being totally impossible.

"You just have to wait—you know I'll tell you if something happens." Unbelievable!

I got mad and said, "Well, good luck with your carp (some sort of bottom-sucking fish?)." Then I hung up.

Now I'm kind of wishing I hadn't said that.

What a dumb put-down!

Maybe she didn't hear it.

Maybe I can fix it.

Good luck with your . . .

harp.

sharp.

warp.

Who Are You?

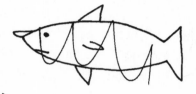

I used to think I was "good at drawing" until I met Sandra. She knows how to draw in perspective and make things look real. I'm more of a cartoon-type artist, which is okay, but it's not the kind of art you'd want to frame.

Chapter 10

THURSDAY

FORGIVENESS

It's one of those warm, fuzzy words that seems so greeting-card perfect, sweet, safe ... but it's really hard to do. Generally, there's probably a huge line at the "I'd like some forgiveness" store and only one person working at the cash register—kind of like at Blockbuster.

And people in line can get awfully grumpy.

It seems like a lot more work and effort for the person doing the forgiving, so the one getting the forgiveness should try to be appreciative!

CRUSH

Sometimes you get a crush on someone you thought you would never look twice at. Most often this happens when your potential crush is too ordinary or too special.

Definition of "Too Ordinary"

A guy who is just a friend.

A guy who you occasionally see. Like the guy who works Saturdays at the grocery store.

A guy who is just friends with one of your friends.

Definition of "Too Special"

A guy who is popular at school and who you know would never even notice you in a million years. He's easy to have a crush on but you know better than to let it happen because nothing will ever come of it.

A guy who is famous.

A guy who is a lot older than you.

A guy who is crazy good-looking (why even try).

Generally, the best way to have relationship success is to be realistic, but there are always exceptions. That's what everyone is really hoping for—an exception.

PRINCE ON HORSE

i saw Sandra this morning and said, "How's your musical heart?"—which was a totally _____ (lame, stupid, dumb, really really idiotic, pathetic, moronic, etc.) thing to say. I was trying to find a way to reference the conversation back to last night's phone call so I could say, "I didn't say carp! I said harp, as in love song. You know, angels and hearts and stuff."

Sandra gave me her do-you-think-I'm-a-total-idiot look and said, "The carp is a very beautiful fish!" And then she did that tsking thing with her mouth and walked off. I spent the rest of

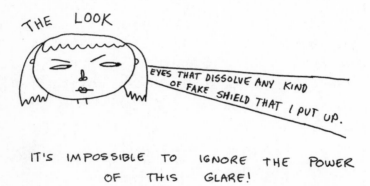

THE LOOK

EYES THAT DISSOLVE ANY KIND OF FAKE SHIELD THAT I PUT UP.

IT'S IMPOSSIBLE TO IGNORE THE POWER OF THIS GLARE!

the day with the Sarahs, trying to avoid Sandra so she couldn't ignore me. Not so hard to do if the person you are avoiding is your best friend—you pretty much know her schedule.

I could tell that Sarah J. had told Sarah W. about the Andrew thing (so much for secrets) because Sarah W. kept bringing up Andrew Wright and then saying slightly negative things about him. Like she expected me to rush to his defense and prove my "love." I tried to pretend I didn't know that she knew I supposedly liked Andrew, but she was really working it.

THINGS YOUR FRIENDS MIGHT DO
TO CRUSH-TEST YOU

WHAT THEY SAY	YOUR LIKE-HIM REACTION
I saw Andrew* today.	Oh really. Who was he with? What was he doing? Did you talk to him? (plus any other questions you can think of)
Don't you think that Andrew* guy is a little moody?	Really? Why do you say that? He seems really nice to me. He's always so friendly . . . (and then you go on about his positive attributes for twenty minutes.)
I think (name of another girl) has a crush on Andrew.*	You go completely nuts, get upset and ask 20 million questions.
I was talking to Andrew* and he asked about you.	You go completely nuts and ask twenty million questions.
I think that Andrew* is kind of cute.	You either come clean about your crush and claim the guy or you run the risk of your friend saying she likes him, and then it's too late.

* USING THE NAME ANDREW JUST AS AN EXAMPLE.

I was trying to be cool and not say anything but after a while I got tired of it and said, "Andrew this, Andrew that? Can we please talk about something else?" Normally, I wouldn't be this snippy with Sarah W., but I was upset about the Sandra fish thing.

And then, before she had any time to say anything back, Andrew walked up and said, "Hi." He looked at me and then at Sarah W. I couldn't believe it!

I don't think she could either—she's not used to getting the second look. I just nodded my head and smiled in a (hopefully) not completely stupid way. Nobody said anything. We all just stood there, and then Andrew said, "Yeah, well, I've got to go. See ya."

Sarah W. answered back, and said, "Yeah, I'll see you in math class," but it was my "see ya!"

Andrew definitely noticed me! He was looking extra cute too— like he just came in from outside, with his brown hair a little mussed up and his jacket under his arm. I swear he could have been in a TV ad. Sarah W. gave me the "not bad" eye look. Sometimes if a guy is super cute you just have to acknowledge it—no matter what's happened.

THINGS GUYS DO THAT MIGHT MEAN
THEY LIKE YOU

Talk to you first when you are with a group of people.

Ask you a question about an assignment or test when they could ask one of their friends.

Smile or give you a raised eyebrow hello every time they pass you.

Come up and talk to you when you are with your friends.

Ask you casually if you are going to be at an event. For example: "Are you going to that music thing?"

Remark that they went somewhere and didn't see you there. For example: "I went to that music thing . . . I didn't see you there."

Tell you casually that they are going somewhere in the hope that you will go too. For example: "I'm going to go to that music thing."

Of course, the big danger is that guys do pretty much the same stuff when they like someone like your best friend. It's a way for them to get to the best friend through you. That's why you have to be careful and fully analyze the situation before you get all excited or worse, make a complete fool of yourself. So does this mean . . .

I've got to make up with Sandra! It's no fun liking someone and not being able to talk about it.

Do I really like him? A pre-crush? Do I have a real crush?

LATER

I phoned Sandra and left her a message. She probably knew it was me and didn't want to pick up. I read her a list of the positive attributes of the carp, which was not very easy to put together. The carp as a fish is not so amazing.

POSITIVE ATTRIBUTES OF THE CARP

Puts up a pretty good fight if caught.

Can live for over forty years.

Is originally from Asia.

Koi carp, which are bred by the Japanese, are actually very
   beautiful.

Carp tongue was considered a delicacy during the Middle Ages.

(I thought Sandra might like this since she eats those disgusting meat sandwiches.)

I was hoping she'd know I'd sacrificed myself and gone down to
the dungeon with the spiders and mice to get this information off
the computer. I wouldn't go down there for just anybody. I couldn't
believe she didn't call me right back. Sandra has one of those
phones where the light blinks to tell you there is a message. I kept
checking my phone every couple of minutes to make sure it was
still working. Finally, after about twenty-three minutes, she called.
Right away she said, "You owe me! Who were you talking to? Your
line was busy."

I answered, "Absolutely!" and "My mom—she was too lazy to
walk up the stairs and nag" (white lie). Sometimes it's better
not to tell everything about yourself, especially if it makes you
seem kind of desperate. The good thing about Sandra is that
she doesn't like to talk things to death. She didn't even bring
up the carp thing. Mostly we talked about the French shoe
project. Sandra wants to have the shoes talking about the people who are wearing them. My shoes would have a lot to say
about me. "She's crazy! Let us go! Donate us to the needy!

We'd rather be homeless!" That's probably why I'm not so sure about her idea. I decided to save the Andrew story until tomorrow. I didn't want her to think I was just making up with her so that I could talk about myself . . . which I wasn't, but still. I could hardly stand it. Sometimes I really have an amazing amount of self-control!

ANDREW WRIGHT LOOKED AT ME!
ANDREW WRIGHT SPOKE TO ME!
ANDREW WRIGHT LIKES ME!

ME IF I HAD NO SELF-CONTROL

Chapter 11

MONDAY

WISH

That good things stay good.

That bad things change.

ORBS OF FATE

STATE OF ME

← REALLY GOOD ORB (VERY, VERY RARE)

← REALLY BAD ORB

As per this diagram, I can't have all good. Really the best I can hope for is limited bad, but what I'll probably get is a whole mess o' bad.

*This took a really long time to draw.

GAMES

I don't like playing board games. I think it's because nobody seems to take it as seriously as I do. I mean, if you are going to sit there and commit three hours to playing, you should at least try. Sandra is the worst. I will never play Monopoly with her again—you can't just suddenly announce, "I'm tired of this, let's do something else" the moment you land on someone's property with three hotels. And then on top of that, she said she couldn't understand why I was so UNREASONABLY upset. It gets me mad just writing about it. I love Sandra, but sometimes I just hate her too!

Mike and I play this silly note game where he puts notes in my locker, and I try and guess who he's writing about. It's kind of like twenty questions. I used to think it was really fun, but lately I'm not so into it. I shoved the latest ones on my top shelf to read later, but I'll probably just throw them away. You'd think he'd clue in and stop sending them since they aren't getting answered . . . but no.

I'm obviously going to have to make some kind of formal let's-not-do-that-note-thing declaration. And then he'll get all weird on me and ask me why. Why can't people be just a little bit psychic?

Sarah J. sat with Sandra and I during lunch, so I had to wait until after school to give Sandra the full Andrew update. She smiled and said, "SEE," like she knew what was going to happen all along. It felt a little unfair that she had my crush information but wasn't going to tell me hers, but I didn't say anything about it. I wanted to be friends with Sandra more than I wanted to know who she maybe might sort of like. Not that it isn't driving me crazy not to know. The Sarahs have been so friendly and nice. Sarah W. told me that she thought Sandra was offbeat stylish in a good way, which is nicely weird because those two hardly ever say nice things about each other. I can't explain or understand it. If they just got to know each other a little bit better, I'm sure they could be friends. I think it's mostly Sandra's fault— she's got some kind of Sarah W. friendship blockage. Sandra came over after school and we tried to work on our French shoe project. Right away I could tell that Sandra just wanted to draw nice pictures of shoes and leave all the words and story parts for me to figure out—but we worked it out when I suggested that maybe I should draw the shoes. She's kind of picky about artistic things.

MY THREE DRAWINGS OF SHOES

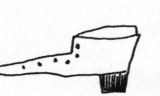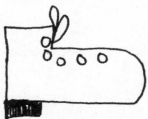

Then out of the blue, when we were having a banana bread snack (with walnuts of course) she said, "How come you aren't answering Mike's notes anymore?" I couldn't believe that he had complained to her. What a baby!

"It takes too long to write notes all the time. I'm just not into it anymore. Did he say anything else?" I was trying to be carefully curious.

"No. So you're not mad at him or anything, right?" Sandra just seemed to want to make sure we were still friends—that everyone was happy.

So I said, "No, I'm not mad at him."

I thought it was all taken care of but then Sandra said, "You should probably tell him that you don't want to play the note game anymore. Do the official game-breakup thing."

I was confused. "The game-breakup thing?" Sometimes Sandra makes up her own rules.

"Like breaking-up-with-a-boyfriend-but-you're-breaking-up-with-a-friend-game." I couldn't believe it.

"Come on, Sandra, you're not serious!" I said.

She was unmoved. "What's the big deal? It'll be like practice for when you have to break up with a real boyfriend. All you have to do is tell him in person." Suddenly Sandra is all persnickety about doing the right thing? She said she and Mike had talked while she was waiting for me and he had seemed upset, so she thought I should do something about it. I guess she was sort of right. This would have been a perfect time to say something back to her about trying to be nicer to Sarah W., but I didn't think about it until later. I'm always missing good comeback opportunities.

I guess she was right. I had to do something.

WHO CAN YOU IGNORE?

SOMEONE YOU HARDLY EVER SEE?	Yes
SOMEONE WHO YOU SEE TWENTY TIMES A DAY BECAUSE THEIR LOCKER IS RIGHT NEXT TO YOURS?	No

It's easy to be fun and jokey with people but not so easy to be serious and truthful.

Mom came up and asked Sandra if she wanted to stay for dinner. She really likes Sandra. Sandra said she wished she could but that Claire was making dinner and she had to go home to show support for Claire's cooking effort. In other words, her mom had said she had to be home. Poor Sandra. Then Mom asked about Sandra's job, which was totally sneaky. She thinks I should have a regular Saturday job too. She had to work when she was my age so she wants me to suffer as well. She says it builds character and money appreciation, but I think it's just because her parents made her do it. You'd think she'd be more sensitive since she spent her weekends working, but she's not—she just wants to pass on the misery. The whole time Sandra was telling her

MISERY

WAIT UP! I'VE BEEN SENT TO MAKE YOUR LIFE MISERABLE.

how much she liked her job, Mom kept giving me the see-you-should-be-like-her look. It wasn't Sandra's fault. She has a great job—of course she likes it. As soon as Sandra saw what Mom was doing she changed the subject back to Claire and her horrible cooking, but it was too late. Mom had to tell Sandra all about the great job she could get me at the library if only I would call Mrs. Wilson's son, Paul. He works at the library and is suppose to have all kinds of connections in the hiring department. I don't even know him, plus I think he might be kind of old and dorky. What could Sandra do? She had to say something. She said, "Libraries are interesting." It was a real general nothing statement, but Mom jumped all over it.

She said, "You're right Sandra, I think it sounds like an interesting job too!" then she crossed her arms and looked at me.

I wanted to yell at her and say "SANDRA DIDN'T SAY THE JOB WAS INTERESTING, SHE SAID LIBRARIES ARE INTERESTING. IT'S LIKE SAYING THE SKY IS BLUE, CLOUDS MEAN RAIN, GUYS LIKE BOOBS; WHY CAN'T YOU LISTEN FOR ONCE!" But I didn't. Instead I said, "Okay, okay, I'll call next week." I'm such a wimp!

Mom said, "Great!" and then squeezed Sandra's shoulder and gave her a whispered "Thank you." It was horrible, sneaky, and manipulative! I could tell that Sandra thought I would be mad at her, but I wasn't. After years of experience with Mom, I know how she operates.

OPERATION MANUAL FOR MoM

RULE 1

USE ANYTHING AND EVERYTHING TO GET YOUR WAY.

RULE 2

ALWAYS USE RULE 1

When Mom left Sandra said, "I'm so sorry! I can't believe what just happened!" I was mad, but I couldn't be mad at Sandra so I just stood there not knowing what to do. It seemed like forever and then Sandra said she had to go or she'd be late for dinner. I knew she wanted to say or do something to make me feel better, but sometimes it's better to just do nothing. Sandra left and I lay on the bed and cried, getting wet stains all over my favorite yellow pillow. I'm an emotional super bouncy ball—bouncing all over the place at top speed and never quite knowing where I'm going to end up.

I didn't feel like eating dinner. I didn't feel like

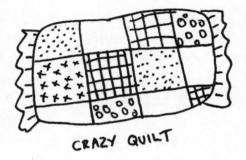

YELLOW PILLOW

CRAZY QUILT

being with Mom and Dad. Every time Mom looked at me, I just glared back or pretended not to notice her—I'm getting good at this. Thankfully, she didn't say anything about the job. Finally, she stopped trying to include me in the conversation, and she and Dad chatted about his day at work, which was boring and didn't involve me.

LATER

About an hour after dinner, Dad came upstairs and knocked on my door. He said he wanted to have a talk. Usually that's not a good thing so I was bracing myself to get in trouble. (Besides, Dad's not one for bedside chitchats.) Surprise! He wasn't mad at me at all! He asked me if I thought I could be patient with Mom because she was having some issues. He wanted me to try and be nicer to her, stuff like that. At first it sounded like he was saying I was the cause of all her grief so I started to defend myself, but he stopped me and went into this whole thing about how he wasn't a psychologist so this was just his opinion blah, blah. Finally, he said he thought Mom was having a bit of a pre-midlife crisis, even though technically she isn't middle aged yet. He said he thought she was a little envious of ME! Something about her insides not matching up with her outside—still feeling young but being old. Stuff like how I can eat a ton of sweets and not gain weight while Mom eats two donuts and can't fit into her pants. He said we needed to show Mom we loved her just the way she was. Then he patted my shoulder and left the room. It was the strangest conversation we've ever had: first because he never talks about feelings and secondly because I didn't think he cared so much about Mom. I suppose I'll try and be more friendly with Mom and maybe lay off the treats if she can see me eating them—

REGULAR LENGTH ARMS

MONKEY LENGTH ARMS

SUBTLE BUT IMPORTANT DIFFERENCE

I'm lucky I've got Dad's metabolism. Too bad you can't pick and choose which bits you'd like to have from each parent. I'd give back Dad's long monkey arms and take Mom's normal ones instead. In fact, there's a whole list of trade-ins but I'm not going to get into it now. Poor Mom.

Chapter 12

SATURDAY

JOB

My Bad-Luck Job

Sandra works Saturday mornings for a company that helps old people. Every Saturday she visits with Mr. Dennis and Mr. And Mrs. Wong. She takes Mr. Dennis to the grocery store. She says he is very funny and sweet and always gives her a piece of fruit to take home. After Mr. Dennis, she goes to visit with the Wongs. Mr. And Mrs. Wong set the table with their fancy china and always serve interesting Chinese pastries for treats. She says the only bad part is washing up the dishes—she's a little nervous she'll break something. But other than that, she loves her job. Since Sandra's job was so great, I decided I would sign up with the old-people company too—I like my grandpa. They gave me Mrs. Swinton and Mr. Robertson. As soon as I met Mrs. Swinton, I knew it was going to be a disaster. She had me clean her entire apartment. Even the bathroom—which is something I don't even have to do at home! Not only that, but she was real grumpy and picky and kept telling me that the last girl had stolen all her sponges. I don't even know how to describe Mr. Robertson because I couldn't see him. His apartment was super dark and he just sat on his sofa and wouldn't even talk to me. I left after ten minutes. It was too creepy. Mom was surprisingly understanding and said, "Old people can be difficult."

TOILET BRUSH

PET PEEVES

My List Of The Sort Of Annoying

- Leftovers served up for dinner. If you didn't eat it all up on the first night, it probably wasn't that good.
- People who throw garbage out of their car. Cigarettes count!
- People who give you way too much information when all you wanted was a short answer to a simple question. Teachers just love to do this. They love the sound of their own voices. Maybe that's why they became teachers.
- Cats that seem friendly but then hiss when you get close enough to pet them, especially if someone else is watching you. It's dishonest and sneaky!
- Dog poop on the sidewalk. If people have a dog, they should clean up after them. It's almost impossible to get it off your shoe if you are wearing shoes with a grooved surface, and what shoes don't have a grooved surface—slippers?
- Driving with Dad and how he beeps the horn for the slightest thing, and not a friendly beep-beep, but a press-on-the-horn-for-twenty-seconds beep. It's I-wish-I-was-invisible embarrassing!

I'M FRIENDLY.

i met Sandra at the mall for lunch after her Saturday job. She wants me to try again with the old-people job. She said her boss was really sorry that it hadn't worked out and told her they would reassign me to new people if I wanted to give it another try. I guess Mrs. Swinton has gone through a lot of helper girls—they said she's not an easy customer. I told Sandra I'd think about it, but I'm not sure I'm enough of a people person for the job. Plus, it's not like I'd be working with Sandra—I don't think two helpers can work for the same client. What's the chance that I would get assigned to great people like Mr. Dennis and the Wongs? Probably none. I told her about my conversation with Dad. She thought it was strange too. Her mom probably isn't going to have a midlife crisis because she's still really hot-looking, whereas Mom just looks like a regular mom. It'll be a long time until they do the mom-daughter envy-thing switch—Sandra's got a little way to go until she looks as great as her mom.

Sandra said she wasn't very hungry but would be into sharing something. She was probably full of Chinese pastries. I said I was going to have a turkey burger but would share my fries if she wanted. You have to be careful with your food around her. She always says she's not hungry but then ends up eating most of your lunch.

After lunch we just kind of wandered around. It can be fun to shop even when you don't have any money. Sandra loves to play the French shopping game in expensive stores. It makes me a little bit nervous because it's hard not to laugh when you're making things up. Sandra pretends to be my French cousin who doesn't speak English, and I am the translator who tells the shopping clerk what she is saying. Of course we have to be careful and not

THIS MEANS "HELLO, I AM FRENCH."
BUT WHAT IT REALLY MEANS IS "HELLO,
I AM SUPER COOL AND INTERESTING
BECAUSE I AM FROM ANOTHER COUNTRY."

pick anyone who can really speak French—not really that hard to do. We usually say that Sandra is looking for an outfit for a wedding or a fancy party. The best part is that the shopping clerks really seem to get into it. They get all excited that they have a real French customer. Of course we never buy anything . . . but it's fun to make Sandra try on all sorts of outfits. Sandra is tall, so most of the stuff she tries on looks good on her. Tall is good—I wouldn't mind growing a few more inches.

Today we went into Dyliss (the new pricey clothing store next to the bookstore). But before I even had a chance to translate, the store clerk spoke to Sandra in French. Thank God Sandra can fake a French accent! We left the store before she figured out what was going on. Sandra told her that she had to use the washroom and that we would come back; of course we didn't. Then we spent about an hour picking out shoes that we would buy if we had the money. In the last shoe store, I tripped over a shoe on the floor and bashed my leg on that little stool thing that the shoe person sits on. Nobody but Sandra seemed to care that I was lying on

SHOE STORE STOOL

WHERE THE SHOE SALESPERSON SITS.

PLACE FOR YOUR FOOT

the ground in pain. They have really bad service there—cute shoes, but bad service. As we were leaving, Sandra said, "You could sue them," in a really loud voice, but I don't think they cared. Maybe they could tell we weren't going to buy anything. I limped over to one of the benches they have in the middle of the mall.

My leg was really hurting!

I was inspecting the wound—no blood but definitely a bruise, when I heard Sandra say, "Hi." It was Jason. How odd. We told him about the shoe store, but I think he thought it was weird that we were in the store pretending to shop when we weren't really going to buy anything. He seemed extra chatty with Sandra and asked her about her self-portrait. The last time we'd seen him, Sandra had told him she was doing a self-portrait in art class. She said she thought it sounded intriguing—I guess she was right since he remembered. We talked some more, and then Jason said he had to go because he was going to see a movie. It was some kind of action thing that I had never heard of before. Then we all stood there not saying anything. It seemed like he didn't really want to leave or was waiting for us to say something.

So I said, "Sandra and I really like movies too." Not the most brainiac thing to say, but no one else was talking.

I guess Jason thought I was trying to get us invited along because he said, "I kind of have to go alone with my dad." Sandra stepped in and saved the day. Maybe I should get her a Lycra cape and a mask.

OH, WE WEREN'T INVITING OURSELVES ALONG. WE JUST LIKE MOVIES.

I'M HERE TO SAVE THE DAY!

When Jason was finally gone, I knew Sandra would just be going nuts. As he was walking away he said, "Maybe we can catch a movie sometime. If you wanted, you know. Okay. See ya." He definitely likes her! Wow! It was like we were both having crush luck at the same time—and that never happens!

BENEFIT OF CRUSH LUCK AT THE SAME TIME

You can talk freely and often about how happy you are without worrying about hurting your friend's feelings because she doesn't have what you have.

"Oh my God, Sandra! He totally likes you!" I was jumping up and down even though my leg hurt like crazy. And then Sandra completely shocked me.

She said, "Did you see his jacket? It had those gross elastic cuffs and waistband. I could never go out with someone who wears that."

"What!" I shouted. I mean, I really shouted—a bunch of people looked at us. "But what about his nice brown jacket? You liked that one." I couldn't even believe we were having this argument. It was like Sandra had turned into some kind of weird style freak. Then she went into a long explanation about pet peeves and how sometimes they just change every-thing. She said her mom had a thing about elastic expandable watch straps and that her dad was not allowed to wear them.

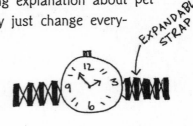

I couldn't believe what I was hearing. Everyone has pet peeves—I'm not an idiot, but this was unbelievably extreme. Sandra was saying that her whole family had some kind of freaky hate thing with elastic. Some arguments are too stupid to even continue so I said, "Whatever!" and stomped (limping) off.

Sandra chased me down, not so hard to do—I was moving pretty slow—and apologized for being so weird. She said she would try and get over the jacket thing. I wanted to help her so I said, "Maybe Jason had to wear it because his dad gave it to him. His parents are divorced."

"Maybe," said Sandra, but I could tell that she was going to write him off. I guess she didn't really like him that much if a crummy jacket had so much power. Sandra tried to make me feel better by asking about Andrew. Like there was any new news since we had talked about him at lunch. I didn't say anything, but I was really disappointed in her. Not so much for not liking Jason but for being so shallow about it all. It was disappointment all around.

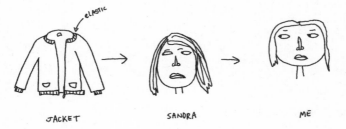

JACKET → SANDRA → ME

We took the bus home and talked about the shoe project. I don't think it's going to be as easy as we originally thought. It's hard to make things funny. Sandra went home instead of coming over like we had originally planned. She said she forgot that she needed to help Claire with something, and I was glad she made up an excuse to leave. I needed at least a whole night to get over her weirdness. Mom asked about Sandra and then said, "She's so devoted to her sister—that's nice," when I said she had gone home to help Claire. We had a nice dinner and an amazing nut-free dessert (an apple-tart thing). I guess Mom bought it because Sandra was supposed to be here. I ate her piece too! Mom and Dad seem to be getting along better.

1   2   ③   4   5

(Chapter 13)

SUNDAY

DREAM

There are people who dream about celebrities—but not me. My dreams just seem to be a weirder continuation of my life: sort of satisfying but always kind of cloud covered.

Like the time I dreamed I was flying. It should be great to dream you're flying. You get to go all over and see all sorts of things, but not me. Here I was doing this really cool thing, but I was just in my bedroom bumping up against the ceiling like a balloon. I couldn't even leave the room.

Dad has this book that says if you concentrate really hard, you can make yourself dream about anything you want. The book says it helps if you write down what you want to dream about and then put it under your pillow. I'll have to think of something important to dream about.

LOVE

It's weird how people with kids hardly ever seem like they are in love—even on TV. They are always yelling and upset about something, like they might be on the verge of splitting up. Is love for the young and the very old* only?

YOUNG PEOPLE

PEOPLE WITH KIDS

OLD PEOPLE

*Old couples often look like they might still be in love, or at least happy to be together.

What do I know about love? I can't even get through two weeks of consistent "like"!!

i woke up this morning, and I wasn't mad at Sandra anymore. It was the first thing I thought about, but I was over being mad. I called her after breakfast, but her mom said she had already left the house. I thought she was going to come over and surprise me, but she never showed up. Mom and Dad said they were going for a walk around the Botanic Gardens. At first I said I didn't want to go, but then they said they were only going for a couple of hours, plus they were going to have lunch there. We hardly ever go out to eat, and I didn't really want to stay home all by myself, so I tagged along. I suppose there are worse ways to get a fancy lunch than to look at a bunch of flowers.

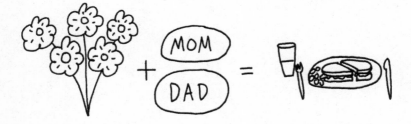

We were just walking along a path under some trees when I noticed that Mom and Dad were holding hands! OH MY GOD! It was so freaky I didn't know what to do. Dad was telling some stupid joke, but I couldn't even hear it—it was like my ears were buzzing with the shock. I just wanted to shout, "WHY ARE YOU HOLDING HANDS? YOU NEVER HOLD HANDS. THIS IS SO WEIRD! DON'T YOU THINK THIS IS WEIRD?" Of course I pretended not to notice, but it was pretty hard to do. I mean, I guess

I was glad that they liked each other, but it just didn't seem like something Mom and Dad would do.

I couldn't wait for them to stop. They held hands right up until we went into the restaurant. I thought I would die! Lunch was okay, but I was really distracted so it was hard to enjoy it that much. After lunch they were their normal selves again, and I was glad when Dad said it was time to go home. I'm a freak—most people would love that their parents were into each other.

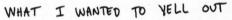

WHAT I WANTED TO YELL OUT

I told Sandra about it later when she called. She said, "Come on, Emily, it's romantic. Sometimes you are so judgmental and weird." I knew she was right, but it sounded a little fishy after that whole elastic-cuff thing.

After we talked, she came over and we worked on our French comic. I think it's going to be kind of cool. I really wanted to do teachers' shoes talking about how horrible the teachers are, but Sandra said Mademoiselle Swanson might show it around in the staff room, which would not be so great for us.

When Sandra left, I practiced the clarinet for sixty-five minutes and near the end I was sounding pretty good. Mom came to my room and asked what song I was playing because she really liked it. I don't know if she was just saying that to make me feel good, but she seemed pretty happy. She sat on my bed, and we just talked about stuff for about twenty minutes. It's been ages since she's done that. It was nice. Maybe Mom and Dad should hold hands more often. I'm not used to thinking about them liking each other so much. I hope they don't start making out. Yuck!

MY CLARINET

Chapter 14

MONDAY

DISAPPOINTMENT

No matter how much you prepare yourself for disappointment, it still affects you! There is always a little piece of you that holds out hope that everything will turn out all right, no matter how much you tell yourself, "Don't get excited because this isn't going to work out."

I was going to fill out this card with all the things that I have been disappointed about but then realized that that would be too depressing, and I'm already not feeling that great.

SAD FACES WITH EARS

During band class, Sarah J. asked me to meet her outside by the front door at lunchtime. This was strange because we always meet in the small lunchroom (A special room that they only open at lunchtime. It has a few comfy chairs and a sofa, so you have to get there right away to get a good spot.), and it was cold outside. I was freezing because I didn't go to my locker to get a sweater. Right away Sarah said she was sorry, so I knew it was going to be something bad. She said that she heard from "someone" that there was a rumor going around that Andrew had a crush on Sarah W. She said that Sarah W. thought that Andrew was cute and nice and everything but that she didn't like him back because the timing was all wrong—whatever that means. My head started to get stuffy, and I had trouble concentrating on what she was saying so I can't exactly remember everything. But what more was there to know? Sarah said she knew how much I liked Andrew, then she went into this whole thing about how hard it is to like someone when they don't like you back. Like we were going to be best friends because we were losers in love. I just wanted to get away from her; my head was buzzing. I told Sarah that I needed to be alone, and she looked at me in such an I'm-so-sorry-for-you way that I almost started to cry. As I was walking away, she ran up to me and gave me a hug. I was totally fine until she did that—it made me tear up, but I don't think she noticed.

I went behind the school where no one could see me and actually cried for the Andrew thing and everything else bad and uncomfortable in my life. I was surprised about how sad I was about Andrew—I guess I didn't know I liked him that much. Luckily, I had the rest of the lunch hour to calm down and try and get my eyes not to be so red. The afternoon was a blur. I saw Mike at my locker, and he said Sandra was worried and looking for me because I hadn't turned up at lunchtime. Without even thinking, I told him that I didn't want to do the note-game thing anymore. It came out just like that. "I'm sorry, I don't want to play the note game anymore."

Mike said, "Sure," like he didn't even care about it. And there it was, over and not a big deal. I guess I was feeling so blah I couldn't get worked up about something else.

After school I told Sandra what Sarah J. had said. I was surprised at how calm I was; I didn't cry or stutter or anything. Sandra freaked out! She was almost like one of those cartoon characters on TV where their ears smoke and then their head blows up. She said, "It's just like Sarah W. to take everything for herself! I don't know how you can stand her! She's . . ." then she rattled off a whole list of nasty things about Sarah. Most of them weren't true, but somehow it made me feel a little better. It's always more satisfying to be mad than sad. At the corner store (that's where Sandra has to turn off to get to her house), she said she'd call me later and then a half-block later yelled, "Sarah W. stuffs her bra!" It was so silly and stupid that it made me smile almost all the way home—I guess Sandra really does have boob envy. Nothing much new happened at home. Mom and Dad still seemed friendly and we had another NUT-FREE tart for dessert. I guess Mom has given up on losing weight.

CHOOSE ONE

HAPPY AND FAT   GRUMPY AND THIN

LATER

I'm not sure what to think about the whole Andrew–Sarah W. thing. Who wouldn't like her? She's cute, pretty, and nice, plus she has great boobs. You really can't blame someone for liking someone can you? I mean they can't help it—it's nature. Besides, it's not like Sarah likes him back. It's not fair for me to be mad at Sarah W. I don't want to turn into Sandra.

- SCENARIO ONE
  Sarah W. is wrong and Andrew likes me, not her.
  I am happy.

- SCENARIO TWO
  Sarah W. is right. Andrew is crazy for her, but she
  doesn't like him back.
  Andrew and I are unhappy.

- SCENARIO THREE
  Sarah W. is right. Andrew is crazy in love with her, and
  she secretly likes him too.
  They get together and are happy.
  I am unhappy.

I'm tired of thinking about all this!
I'm stranded on Crush Island!
The crummy thing about this is
that I didn't even like Andrew
until Sandra said he was noticing
me. How committed can I really
be?

Chapter 15

Tuesday

DUTY

"Duty" is one of those words that seems all about having to do something that you would rather not do, but you have no choice, you have to do it—it's your duty. Just like now it's MY DUTY to call about that stupid job at the library. It doesn't sound like a very exciting job— hanging out all by myself quietly shelving books. How fun will that be? Hopefully they won't have some kind of timed alphabet test. I'm not even sure I totally get the Dewey decimal system.

WHICH COMES FIRST?

DW632.HG

DH5994.RA

H63.B9

Some numbers from the library books I had in my room.

I suppose it's also my duty to be nice to Sarah W. I know it's probably not her fault that Andrew might be deeply in love with her, but it would be easier to avoid her than to be friendly and hang out. What if she says something embarrassing to me? Like how sorry she is that Andrew doesn't like me, or how DUMB I am for even thinking that he would.

What a disaster!!!!

FATE

Fate happens no matter how hard you try to stop it. It can be good or bad. Sandra says it was because of fate that we became friends. The evidence is pretty strong.

Sandra's mom and dad had a huge fight about where Sandra should go to school. Sandra's dad won so Sandra went to public school, and her dad bought a new fishing boat with the money he saved from private school. He named it "Suzanne," after Sandra's mom, but she still stayed mad about the school thing.

On the first day of school, my homeroom teacher was sick so they reassigned some of us to other classes that didn't have as many students. When I went into my new homeroom, every seat was taken except for the one next to Sandra and that's how we met!

Unfortunately, fate is one of those things that you don't know is happening to you until after it has happened. While you're in it you ask lots of questions like, Why is this happening? What's going on? Why did this happen? And then when it's all over, you look back and say, "Oh well, I guess it was fate."

Big news for today! Mr. Shapiro and Ms. Clark are putting the gym classes together. We are going to learn how to dance old-people style. Some of the boys at school think that Mr. Shapiro and Ms. Clark have a love connection, which I'm sure they don't. First of all, Mr. Shapiro is really short and kind of dumpy look-ing—like an ugly elf. And secondly, he is married. Sometimes boys don't clue in that a guy can't just get any girl he wants.

Ms. Clark is so out of Mr. Shapiro's league. She's tall, very pretty, and maybe a lesbian. She has a photo on her desk of her and another woman posing in front of the Eiffel Tower. Janelle, one of the nosy smarty-pants girls in our class, asked if that was her sister, and Ms. Clark said no, it was her roommate. Janelle tried to start a whole Ms. Clark–is-a-weirdo-lesbian rumor, but Carol put a stop to it right away. Carol said that she thought les-bians were cool and that anyone who made fun of them was shal-low and a discriminator, and then she looked right at Janelle, so there was no doubt about who she was talking about. Of course, Janelle shut right up. I used to think that Carol was sort of stuck-up and snobby (she's really rich and popular and on the volley-ball team), but maybe I was wrong. If I were a lesbian I'd pick a girlfriend who was exactly my size so we could share clothes. Maybe that's why Ms. Clark has such an amazing wardrobe.

At first I thought the only good thing about the dancing class was that we didn't have to wear our whole gym outfit, just our gym shoes, but there was more. When we first got to the gym, everyone stood around not knowing what to do. Mr. Shapiro said something lame like, "Boys pick your lady," but only Daniel and Samantha paired up. (Easy for them, they have been going out forever.) After about five minutes, when the music was all ready,

Mr. Shapiro told the boys he would pick their partners if they didn't want to. This got everybody moving. I couldn't believe that Andrew walked over to me. He moved his eyebrows to say, So do you want to do this together? I nodded yes.

"What do you think, troll or elf?" he asked, then he nodded his head toward Mr. Shapiro.

I was worried about my voice being squeaky, but I said, "Elf, definitely elf." Then we both laughed. The dancing lessons were harder than you'd think—I'm not very coordinated. I was glad that I had to concentrate on counting steps because it was so weird to be actually TOUCHING Andrew. It was a definite I-can't-believe-this moment, except that it lasted for forty-five minutes. I was a buzzy-shaky-happy mess. Andrew was so chatty and fun that by the end of class I was hardly nervous anymore. I wish I could remember everything he said. We talked about cameras (he wants to get a new one), turtlenecks (I hate them because they make me feel like I'm choking), socks with holes in the toes (his left sock was really bugging him while we were dancing), and pancakes (we both like them). The last dance we learned was the polka. It was the easiest one, so everyone was having a lot of fun bouncing around the gym. Mr. Shapiro and Ms. Clark were going around asking partners to leave the floor until only the best polka couple was left. Andrew and I were third best.

Andrew said, "Third place still gets a medal," and I was glad that he was happy.

I said, "I'm not sure it's that cool to be really good at the polka anyway."

And he said, "You might be right about that."

At the end of class, Andrew said, "I guess I'll see you on Thursday."

I said, "You bet," which probably was a little too enthusiastic, but I was happy so I don't care. Maybe he'll just think I like dancing. He could have picked any of the popular girls, like Andrea, Grace, or Jennifer, but he didn't! He picked me! I don't get it! Maybe Sarah W. is wrong . . . or maybe he's just being nice and I'm a complete idiot!!!

Of course I told Sandra about it as soon as I could find her. She said it was fate and that fate is very powerful. When I finished telling her everything that Andrew had said, she said that Sarah W. should shut her mouth about things she doesn't know anything about. I didn't say anything out loud, but inside I added an amen. Andrew didn't even ask about Sarah W.

Mom and Dad were oddly happy and nice to each other again. It's like someone slipped them love a potion. Our whole house is in love!

I wrote Andrew's name on a piece of my fancy paper and put it under my pillow.

Maybe I'll dream about him.

Chapter 16

WeDNesDAY

HAPPY MEMORY

A long time ago—before I ever thought that one day I might want a boyfriend—I was playing at the park with Jason and a couple of other kids from the neighborhood. We were playing that tag game where you have to jump on all the playground stuff and aren't allowed to touch the ground or you're out. I was clumsy back then too, so I fell off the monkey bars while I was trying to escape from Kevin, who was It. I tried not to cry, but I couldn't help it. My leg was bleeding and my hands were all cut up. Jason came running over and helped me up. He walked me all the way home and even took off his jacket and put it around my shoulders. I kind of had a little crush on him for a while after that. I don't think he had a crush on me—he was just being nice.

JASON* plus JACKET =

* Which is why I still think Sandra is INSANE!!!

Chapter 16

WeDNesDAY

PETS

We're not really a pet family. Becca thinks it's really weird that we don't have any pets—her family is just crazy for animals. Becca's dad loves their dog, Monte. Sometimes Becca complains that he might even like Monte better than the rest of the family. But Becca's smart, she uses her dad's dog love to get what she wants. Whenever she needs extra money or wants to go somewhere, she asks her dad, not her mom. Like the time she wanted some red boots. I was standing with her, and I couldn't believe it. She said, "Daddy, I need some new boots and I asked Monte and he said I should get them." Then her dad said, "Is this true, Monte?" Of course the dog wasn't talking, but they pretended like Monte had an opinion. In the end, her dad gave her the money.

Good dog, Monte!!!

YES. THE BOOTS ARE A MUST!

i called ABOUT THE LIBRARY JOB TODAY! I thought I'd have to have a long uncomfortable conversation with Mrs. Wilson's son, Paul, but he wasn't even there. The lady who I talked to said she was expecting my phone call earlier in the week—like I had already disappointed them somehow and I didn't even have the job yet. She asked me lots of questions about my past work experience, and then when I was sure she would say, "Thanks, but no thanks," she said I could come in for an interview next Tuesday after school. I guess you don't need specific book experience to work at the library.

When I got off the phone, I realized that I forget to tell her how much I like to read. Oh well, it's a good thing to remember for the interview. All in all, I felt kind of good about the whole thing. Sometimes thinking about doing a thing is actually worse than doing the thing. Of course I would never tell Mom this—she would just die of happiness to have me admit that I was wrong and she was right. I told Sandra about the job interview, and she seemed surprised that I was excited about it. I couldn't blame her after that freak-out the other day. I suppose I overreacted. Oh well, she's used to my roller-coaster ways.

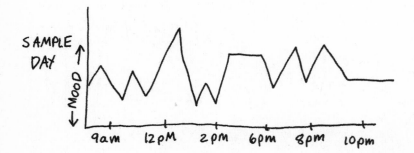

I don't know how some people seem to be so well-adjusted. They never overreact about anything. Becca is kind of like that. It takes a lot to get her worked up. She sees things in perspective right off the bat.

IF LIFE WERE A BOX

HOW I SEE A BOX   HOW BECCA SEES A BOX
(It takes me a long time to see the sides)

I told Sandra I didn't know what to wear to the interview. She said she would help me pick out something library-appropriate.

THiNGS THAT ARE NOT LiBRARY APPROPRiATE

T-SHiRTS, ESPECiALLY
IF THEY HAVE A PiCTURE
ON THEM.

WORN COOL
FADED JEANS

SHOES WiTH CLiCKY
HEELS THAT MAKE
A LOT OF NOiSE WHEN
YoU WALK.

SUPER-SHORT
SKiRTS

FASHION

What People Who Work In Libraries Wear

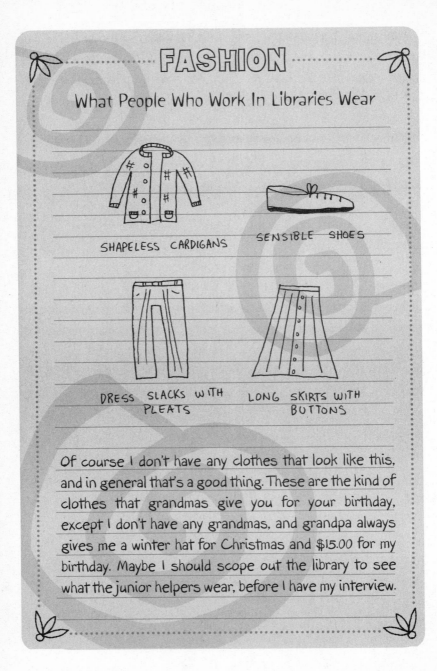

SHAPELESS CARDIGANS

SENSIBLE SHOES

DRESS SLACKS WITH PLEATS

LONG SKIRTS WITH BUTTONS

Of course I don't have any clothes that look like this, and in general that's a good thing. These are the kind of clothes that grandmas give you for your birthday, except I don't have any grandmas, and grandpa always gives me a winter hat for Christmas and $15.00 for my birthday. Maybe I should scope out the library to see what the junior helpers wear, before I have my interview.

Sarah J. has been super friendly the last couple of days. I didn't tell her about being Andrew's partner in dance class because I just know that she would tell Sarah W., and I was worried Sarah W. might say something to ruin it. I'd rather live with the fantasy and be happy than face the reality and be sad.

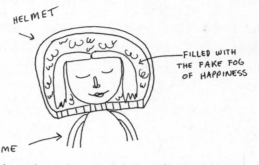

HELMET

FILLED WITH
THE FAKE FOG
OF HAPPINESS

ME

Sarah J. is trying to get me to practice my clarinet more so that I can be a second clarinet like her and then we can sit together. It would be great if I could because she and Martin (the second clarinet next to her) are always joking around, and it looks like a lot of fun. Meanwhile, I'm sitting next to Kevin, who has probably only spoken twelve words to me since the start of the school year—not exactly big fun in the third-clarinet section. I told her I'd try, but I don't think it's going to work out. I'm just not that dedicated.

We don't talk about David specifically (thank God), but Sarah likes to talk about boys in general and most often I think she is talking about David anyway—just in code. She says things like "Don't you think that boys sometimes want something but don't know exactly what it is they want?" It's like she is still holding out hope that David will like her. I suppose it could happen. I've been ignoring him. Every time I see him, I give him my see-through stare like he's invisible and doesn't even exist. I think it's working because now he just looks at the ground or the wall when I walk by. The only annoying thing about hanging out with Sarah is that she feels she has to keep me updated on Sarah W. and Andrew. She said that Andrew always wants to talk to Sarah W. during math class and that yesterday Mr. Stars, the math teacher, almost sent Andrew down to the office for being disruptive. It's as if she thinks if she's super honest, I won't be mad at Sarah W. and blame her because Andrew likes her. All this stuff is too confusing!!! What do I even know about Andrew? Maybe he really does like Sarah W. and is just being nice to me because . . . who knows, to get to her? I'm no love detective!

Here's my pathetic know-nothing survey.

WHAT I REALLY KNOW ABOUT ANDREW

	Yes	No
Where he lives.		X
What he likes to do on the weekends.		X
The name of his best friend—he likes to hang out with James.	X	
If he has any brothers or sisters.		X
His favorite anything . . . food, color, band, TV show.		X
His favorite girl.		XXXX

I ran into Sarah W. in the hall in the afternoon. It was nice, not weird. Now I'm feeling really guilty about all the stuff Sandra was saying the other day. It was crummy of me to play her lets-be-nasty-to–Sarah W. game. Sometimes when you're upset it's so easy to forget what's real and go for what makes you feel better. She made me promise to have lunch with her and Sarah J. tomorrow.

Becca came over after school. Sandra was supposed to come too, but at the last minute she said she had to go home instead. Her mom is making her spend all her free time with Claire. What a drag. It's not her fault that Claire doesn't have any friends! She's just got that weird boyfriend who never talks. Becca knows a little bit about the Andrew thing, but she's not that into boys so I knew she wouldn't want to talk about it. We watched a movie and then she stayed for dinner. Mom surprised me and ordered a pizza. Dad doesn't like pizza but he didn't complain; he just ate some leftovers instead. He always seems happy to be cleaning out the fridge.

Becca's dad came over to pick her up, and I could see Monte sitting in the front seat of the car when her dad honked the horn. Becca says her mom always gets mad that there is fur all over her seat. I guess her dad doesn't care, because when they drove away, Monte was still sitting in the front seat. If you didn't look too closely, you might have thought they were just a happy little family out for a drive.

Tuesdays and Thursdays are my new favorite days.

Chapter 17

THURSDAY

BEST SUPERPOWER

If I could pick any kind of superpower, I'd choose psychic ability. It would make every part of life easier: knowing what other people were thinking so you didn't say the wrong thing at the wrong time, knowing if something unexpected was going to happen so you were ready and waiting for it, and knowing what other people were expecting from you so you didn't disappoint them. Plus, when you lost stuff you could concentrate and then know where to find it. Becca almost seems like she might have psychic ability. She hardly ever gets embarrassed or confused by anything. It's either good to be around her—because she can get you out of trouble—or bad because next to her you look kind of stupid. From the outside it looks likes she doesn't care what she says and somehow it's always the right thing. I asked her

CAPE

LYCRA SUIT

once how she did it, and she looked at me like she couldn't understand what I was talking about.

HA! So maybe she's not so psychic after all.

Other superpowers I might consider include:
- Invisibility (kind of like being psychic, but cheating)
- Photographic memory (so I wouldn't have to study)
- To stop and rewind time (so you could go back and change things if they didn't turn out right)

TALENT

Why are some people good at practically everything they do? It's like they won the I-can-do-anything lottery! And then there are other people who might be good at something, but they can never seem to figure out what that thing might be.

I'm in the no-great-talent category. So far I know I'm not particularly talented at:

- Sports
- The clarinet or singing
- Drawing (I used to think I was good)
- Mind-reading
- Witty, fast comebacks
- Telling jokes or stories
- Public speaking
- Dancing
- Writing and studying
- Friend management
- Persuasive reasoning
- Clue deciphering

I can make a mean stack of banana pancakes. If there's ever a banana pancake emergency, I'm all over it!
This is a skill isn't it?

BANANA PANCAKES

ON PLATE

Of course today was dance class. For some reason, Ms. Clark and Mr. Shapiro decided to change the dance part of the class so that now it's only going to last for half the period. For the last half of the period, we separated into our normal gym classes, which meant that we had to get dressed in our WHOLE GYM OUTFIT!!

Not so great for me since I still had that huge bruise on my leg from the shoe store. I was a little bit nervous that Andrew might pick someone new, but everyone pretty much stuck to the same partners they had in the last class.

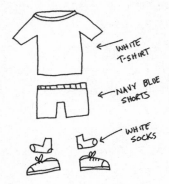

WHITE T-SHIRT

NAVY BLUE SHORTS

WHITE SOCKS

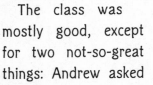

STUPID GYM OUTFIT WE ALL LOOK LIKE CLONES... EXCEPT FOR THE REALLY PRETTY GIRLS. THEY STILL LOOK GREAT.

The class was mostly good, except for two not-so-great things: Andrew asked about the bruise on my leg and if I was good friends with Sarah W. When he asked about the bruise, my face turned bright red—I could feel my ears burning up. I kind of mumbled that I was clumsy and then pretended to be concentrating really hard on the dance we were learning. I'm sure he noticed! Then right before class was over he asked about Sarah W.—right out of the blue—we weren't even talking about friends or anything. I just wanted to die. I said, "I'm having lunch with her today," and I guess he took that as a yes. I thought he was going to go on about how great Sarah W. was, but he didn't say anything more about her. I wasn't very chatty for the rest of the class. I just couldn't think of anything to say.

When class was over, he didn't say, "See you on Tuesday," or "See you next time," or "Have a good weekend." All he said was "Bye." I JUST KNOW I TOTALLY BLEW IT!!!!

Then, to make everything even worse, we had to play volleyball for the last half hour. I hate volleyball! I suck at volleyball! Plus, there are all these girls from the team in our class—so they are really good. It's supposed to be fun, but they get really upset if you miss the ball or hit it out of bounds. (You can just see them looking at each other and rolling their eyes.) I don't think it's fair that we have to play games with people who are practically professionals. By the end of class, I felt like a first-class total loser . . . and then I had to go and have lunch with Sarah W.!

Lunch was okay. I felt a little guilty about not inviting Sandra, though. I told Mike to tell her I had to have lunch with the Sarahs (he always sees her on Thursdays, before lunch, in his art class). The Sarahs didn't talk about Andrew at all. It was like they could tell I was really sad and were being funny and nice, trying to cheer me up. Sarah J. even had brownies—my favorite!!! I wonder if they are mildly psychic—the Sarahs, not the brownies.

I saw Sandra after school and told her what had happened in gym class. She said to try and not read too much into it, but I could tell that she thought it was over. Normally, she would have said something like, "Oh, Emily, just relax—he still likes you!" But she didn't. She didn't say anything like that, and she even changed the subject before I could try and get her to say something else that might make me feel better. She came over, and we worked on the French shoe project. I'm almost finished with my part, but Sandra has hardly done anything. I'm pretty happy with how parts of the quiz turned out. Sandra agreed to let me draw one of the comic panels if I did most of the writing—more work for me, but I don't care. Of course, I had mine all finished and she had hardly started. I got to do the panel about Sandra's mom.

TRANSLATION: "YIPPEE! WE'RE GOING SHOPPING AGAIN!"

Sandra really liked it. She said, "Wow! That looks great Ems!" She hasn't called me that in years. It felt good to have my part all finished.

"Thanks, but you better work on your part over the weekend. It's due next week, you know!"

I guess I was being a little bossy about it because she said, "ALL RIGHT ALREADY!" and then started to pack up her stuff to leave.

Right then I started to cry. I couldn't help myself. Sandra came over, and we sat on the bed together until I felt better. I thought she might think I was upset about the shoe project, but she said, "It's okay to be sad—sometimes love sucks." She's right! LOVE DEFINITELY SUCKS!!!

IMPORTANT CRUSH RULE

Just because a guy is being nice to you does not mean that he LIKES you and that you should suddenly decide that you have a huge crush on him. He is probably just being nice because maybe he is a nice guy.

Sandra stayed for dinner and seemed happy that she was missing a Claire cooking night. Even though Claire is practicing a lot, I don't think she's getting any better. Sandra says she doesn't understand how following a recipe can be so hard. I asked her why Claire was suddenly so into cooking? Sandra shrugged her shoulders and said, "She's going to have to feed a family one day." That made me imagine Claire marrying that goofy boyfriend of hers and having a baby. . . . It just didn't seem possible.

"Poor family." I said it without really thinking.

Sandra laughed and said, "You can say that again."

Mom made chocolate pudding in fancy little glass bowls for dessert. Sandra looked at me across the table like, What, no nuts? It's hard to believe this happy, no-nut Mom is here to stay.

SOMETIMES THINGS TASTE EVEN BETTER WHEN THEY LOOK EXTRA FANCY.

I asked Sandra if she thought Mom looked any fatter. She said she couldn't tell, but that Mom sure seemed to be in a good mood. I said, "Desserts make her happy."

Sandra said, "It's kind of freaky that sugar has so much power."

"You're not kidding!" I said. "Late-night Mom who has had dessert is completely different from late-night Mom who hasn't. I just hope she doesn't balloon up and get one of those pumpkin-type bodies." It's nice to have a friend who fits in with my family and completely gets me.

Chapter 18

FRIDAY

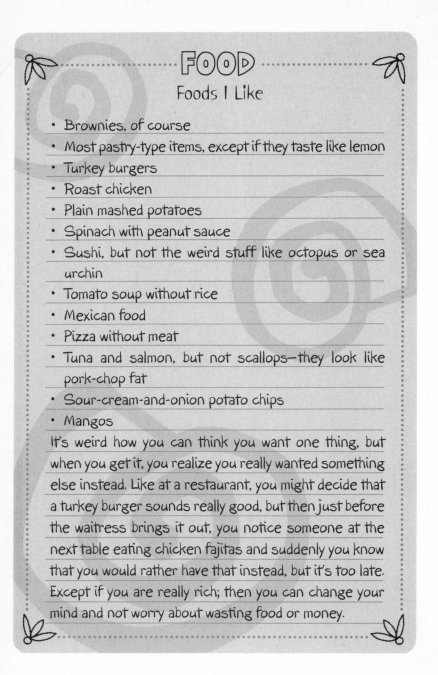

FOOD

Foods I Like

- Brownies, of course
- Most pastry-type items, except if they taste like lemon
- Turkey burgers
- Roast chicken
- Plain mashed potatoes
- Spinach with peanut sauce
- Sushi, but not the weird stuff like octopus or sea urchin
- Tomato soup without rice
- Mexican food
- Pizza without meat
- Tuna and salmon, but not scallops—they look like pork-chop fat
- Sour-cream-and-onion potato chips
- Mangos

It's weird how you can think you want one thing, but when you get it, you realize you really wanted something else instead. Like at a restaurant, you might decide that a turkey burger sounds really good, but then just before the waitress brings it out, you notice someone at the next table eating chicken fajitas and suddenly you know that you would rather have that instead, but it's too late. Except if you are really rich; then you can change your mind and not worry about wasting food or money.

Sandra was waiting at my locker at lunch again today—she's been doing this all week. We usually meet at her locker because it's closer to the small lunchroom. I guess she's just feeling sorry for me—worried that I'll fall apart if I've got to walk downstairs by myself. She and Mike like to joke around a lot, which is good because now I don't think he's mad at me about anything anymore. It's almost like they've become the kind of friends that Mike and I used to be. Generally, today was a nothing day: nothing-happened, nothing-exciting, nothing-nothing. It's weird how I don't ever see Andrew in the halls anymore—just in gym/dance class. Seeing how things turned out, it's probably for the best! Why be uncomfortable and nervous all the time when you can sort of limit it to twice a week? I'm going to go to Sandra's house tomorrow so we can finish off our shoe project.

LATER

Mom rented one of those romantic comedy movies. It was nice to eat brownies and watch the girl get the guy—even if it was only a movie. Makes me feel hopeful and depressed at the same time.

Is this possible? The only bad part was watching the couple making out—that's not something that was completely comfortable with Mom sitting right there.

I think I'm ready to admit that I'm a sweet-aholic. No matter what happens in my life, I'll always have sugar! Yikes—this is probably how Mom thinks . . . SCARY!

I AM THE NO-NUT BROWNIE! I WILL MAKE YOU SMILE.

Chapter 19

SATURDAY

Claire probably had sex with Brad. It's one of those things that Sandra doesn't like to talk about, but it's hard to believe that it didn't happen because once by accident we almost caught them. Claire called Brad her boyfriend, but they only hung out at her house and he never took her anywhere or even introduced her to his friends. One weekend, when Sandra's parents were out of town, Sandra was staying at my house. She forgot her toothbrush so we went back to her house to get it. Brad's car was in the driveway, so we decided to try and spy on them. If you climb on top of the garage you can see right into Claire's bedroom. I'm surprised they didn't hear us climbing, because we could hardly stop laughing. It was uncomfortable weird—Claire had all her clothes off except her underpants, and Brad wasn't wearing his shirt. Sandra just freaked out! She jumped off the garage like a superhero and ran into the house shouting Claire's name. We waited for them in the living room. Claire seemed really nervous, and Brad didn't even look at us; he just left. Sandra went into a whole spiel about how Brad was a complete loser and how Claire should respect herself more and dump him. It was almost as if Sandra were her mom and was telling her off.

SURPRISE

It's weird when the biggest surprises come from your-self. Like all of a sudden, you say or do something totally unexpected. Something that you never thought you would say. It's like you didn't know yourself until you were under pressure, and then you think, Wow, that doesn't seem like me. I didn't know I would do that.

GUESS WHO?

MIRROR

i got to Sandra's house early—about 9:30. Her mom always likes to have lots of different treats available on the weekends. Sometimes she makes these jam-filled things that are just amazing! They have some kind of complicated name that I can never remember. I could tell that I was going to be pastry-lucky as I walked up the driveway. Their house smelled so good.

It's great to have a friend like Sandra—I can just walk into her house and feel completely comfortable. I think it used to kind of make Claire jealous that she didn't really have a best girlfriend, too, but now she has Ian. Ian is her sort of new boyfriend—they were just friends for a long time before they changed over into a romantic couple. Sandra says Ian is really shy but nice once you get to know him. It's hard for me to tell because he always seems so nervous and quiet whenever I see him. He's not very good-looking, but Sandra says he's really smart and is probably going to be a scientist or something one day, so I guess he's a good catch. Claire is secretly knitting him a sweater for his birthday, which Sandra says is a sign of true love because knitting a sweater is way harder than knitting a scarf.

Claire was in the kitchen with Sandra when I walked in. She always gives me a look like, "here comes trouble," and I always say, "Hi, Claire!" like "I can't believe it's you! I'm so happy to see you!" Sandra thinks it's annoying, but we do it anyway.

I took some pastries from the counter, and then Sandra and I went upstairs to work on the never-ending shoe project. It was nice to just hang around on a Saturday morning. Sandra usually has to work on Saturdays, but it was some kind of special old-people holiday so she had the day off. I ate way too many of the jam things—probably because I hardly get to have them anymore, and I had to lie on Sandra's bed for half an hour until I felt better. Sandra asked me how I was feeling and I said, "A little full but okay," which was the right answer to the wrong question. She was asking how I was feeling about Andrew.

Sometimes it's weird how you surprise yourself—like you say something out loud without really thinking and it turns out to be exactly how you feel but you never realized it before. I said I was confused about my real feelings for Andrew, worried that maybe I only liked him because I thought he liked me first—victim of a safe crush. I wasn't sure that I would have even let myself start to like him otherwise: Wasn't he totally out of my league? Sandra didn't have any insightful answers. It seemed like she wanted to tell me something but then changed her mind. It's hard to be wise and smart about love. Sometimes an "oh well" is about the best comment you can come up with.

I wasn't all gloom and doom for the rest of the afternoon, so we had a nice time and actually finished our project. It's amazing! It's like a quiz, with all the answers at the bottom, where you have to guess whose shoes are talking.

Claire was making dinner, so Sandra said it was up to me if I wanted to risk it and stay. She made pizza, and it looked pretty good when she brought it to the table, but I guess she didn't cook it long enough or something because the dough in the middle was soggy and stretchy, so we just ate around the edges. Everyone made a big deal about how the crust was our favorite part so that Claire wouldn't feel bad. She didn't seem too upset, and the cooked part really did taste pretty good. Sandra's mom was worried that we'd all still be hungry, so she whipped up a super-tasty salad when she saw that the pizza wasn't going to work out completely. She's a really good cook. It must drive Claire nuts that she didn't inherit any of her cooking genes.

After dinner, Sandra and I watched a movie. She loves scary movies. I'm such a chicken—I spent most of the movie with my head in a pillow humming so I couldn't hear anything. After it was over, I had Sandra fill me in on all the parts I had missed, which was most of it! She was a good sport and only rolled her eyes twice. I deserved it.

While we were waiting for Dad to pick me up, I asked Sandra if we could pick out my library-interview outfit tomorrow. She said she couldn't because she had to do something with Claire and then Claire walked in the room and said, "Are you two talking about me?" I thought she was just joking, but Sandra got insta-mad and started yelling at her about privacy and minding her own business. It was really weird. Claire looked surprised and mumbled something nasty about Sandra and stomped out. It sure doesn't seem like they should be spending more time together. Poor Sandra. She seemed a little embarrassed about yelling, but you can't really blame her. Claire is sure seeming needy lately, like maybe something bad happened to her again. Dad pulled up right after that so we had a fast good-bye and didn't get to talk about it. Really, I felt kind of sorry for both of them.

LATER

I took the piece of paper with Andrew's name on it and threw it in the garbage. It felt good—I was relieved!

EVEN LATER

Okay. I got out of bed, found the paper in the garbage, and put it back under my pillow. I'M PATHETIC.

Chapter 20

SUNDAY

HOBBIES

- Obsessing
- Reading
- Movies
- Drawing

I can't think of anything else. So far, what I have doesn't sound very impressive. I should take up some kind of new activity.

When I was little, I was really into collecting things. I have all these boxes filled with stuff I used to think was important—stamps; white, round stones; colored beads; funny-looking sticks. They practically take up the entire bottom drawer of my dresser, but I just can't throw them away. Right now it seems like a bunch of junk, but maybe one day I'll decide they're treasures again. It must be a family trait because Mom and Dad just can't throw anything away, either, and they definitely have stuff that is not going to turn into treasures—not in a million years.

They should change the name "hobby". It sounds really dated and frivolous. Like you would expect someone to say, "My hobbies are performing magic tricks and building famous replicas out of Popsicle sticks." It's just too goofy sounding.

Becca came over and we went for a bike ride. She likes to have an activity to do and is not so crazy about just hanging out all the time. I thought I was going to die. It was almost impossible to keep up with her, she goes so fast—especially up hills! She said she couldn't believe how out of shape I was. I said I was a casual cyclist, not an Olympic racer. I guess she took that as a compliment, because she smiled and said, "Thank you." She rode a little bit slower after that, and I was able to keep up and only had to stop to rest at the top of the hills. When we finally got home, my legs were all wobbly and I could hardly walk, which is probably why I tripped over my kickstand when I was putting my bike away. Becca just rolled her eyes as she was helping me up— she thinks I'm a real klutz. She stayed for a couple hours of recovery (mine) and chitchatting, then out of the blue she asked if I knew who Sandra's new crush was. SANDRA'S NEW CRUSH! WHAT NEW CRUSH? I couldn't believe she knew something I didn't! It turns out she was asking about the whole fish-in-the-sea thing. I said it probably hadn't worked out because Sandra had never said anything. But still—weird how I forgot all about it. She said she saw Sandra at the park when she was biking over to my house. She was alone, swinging on the tire swing. They waved at each other, but Becca didn't stop.

"Was she crying?" I was sure something bad had happened between her and Claire. Becca said she couldn't tell, but she thought her hello wave didn't seem especially enthusiastic, like maybe she wasn't super happy that Becca had seen her. We called her, but she wasn't home. Claire said she didn't know where she was and, besides, it wasn't her job to keep tabs on Sandra. She was definitely snippy. It sounded like yet another fight.

LATER

I finally got through to Sandra. All she said was that Claire was a pain, and she didn't want to talk about it. She didn't really want to talk, period, so our entire conversation only lasted about three minutes—a shortness record for us. Older siblings are supposed to make life easier, not harder! If I were brave, I'd talk to Claire and set her straight on some big-sister rules. It's weird how she and Sandra have been fighting so much lately. It reminds me of that whole Brad thing. I wonder if something happened with Ian. Sandra seems to be so mad at her. Like maybe she's gone and gotten pregnant, and that's why she's doing all that cooking stuff . . . so she'll know how to take care of the baby and her boyfriend. Next time I see her I'll have to look at her stomach. How is she going to take care of a baby? She doesn't even know how to babysit!!! Sometimes I just think such crazy thoughts.

Chapter 21

MONDAY

HAPPINESS IS . . .

Hard to Hold On to.

It's difficult not to fall into the trap of thinking if I had only _____ then I would be happy. And then if you get _____ you only end up being happy until you think of _____ and how you now want that, too, and can't possibly be happy until you have it. It's an unfair cycle that's almost impossible to stop. The only time you are truly happy is when you are resting somewhere between having gotten _____ and not yet having thought of _____—the next thing that you decide you want.

Today I am here

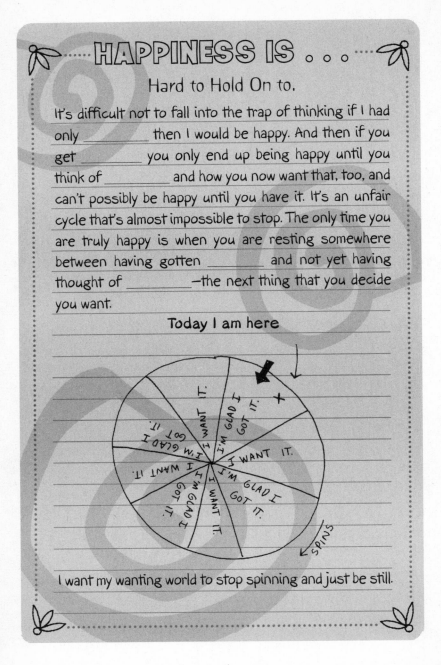

I want my wanting world to stop spinning and just be still.

Sarah J. and Sarah W. invited me to a sleepover at Sarah W.'s house on Saturday night, and they said I could bring Sandra! Wow! Just when you think everything is predictable, something unexpected happens. I couldn't wait to tell Sandra, but it was like she had disappeared off the face of the earth—really frustrating! I knew she was at school, but she wasn't in any of the places she was supposed to be. I was so busy looking for her that I didn't even notice Andrew until he grabbed my arm as I was walking by. He said, "Hi." I said, "Hi," and then he said, "I'll see you tomorrow." Like I wasn't excited enough already! I was in such a good mood I even gave David a smirk when I saw him—probably a big mistake, but I couldn't help sharing the joy.

I was making one more pass by my locker in case she was there waiting for me when Mike asked if I was looking for Sandra. Now he's psychic? He said she was downstairs in Mr. Randolf's, the scary math teacher's office. I waited for her outside the door so Mr. Randolf couldn't see me. I'm glad he's not my teacher! He talks really loudly and always yells out test scores when he's handing back papers. Sandra says he should have probably been an Army teacher or something—nobody likes him.

Sandra finally came out, looking pretty pleased with herself—something about extra credit for getting a problem right. She was so happy I didn't want to mess it up by asking about Claire. Plus, I wanted to get her to come to the Saturday-night sleepover. She wasn't super excited (I knew she wouldn't be) but promised that she would come anyway. I think she is curious about Sarah W.'s house too. I just wanted the day to end there

. . . before anything bad could happen to ruin it. If only I had selective narcolepsy*!!!!!

It's weird to be happy and content but not enjoy it completely because you are worried about when it is going to end. But nothing bad happened. I got to be happy all day.

*That sleeping sickness thing where you instantly fall asleep

Chapter 22

Tuesday

BOYFRIEND

Of course I want a boyfriend—who wouldn't—but somehow I can't even imagine it. It seems like there are about
a million obstacles to pass before it could ever happen.
None of my friends even have boyfriends, and they are
much more together than I am!

BOYFRIEND OBSTACLE COURSE

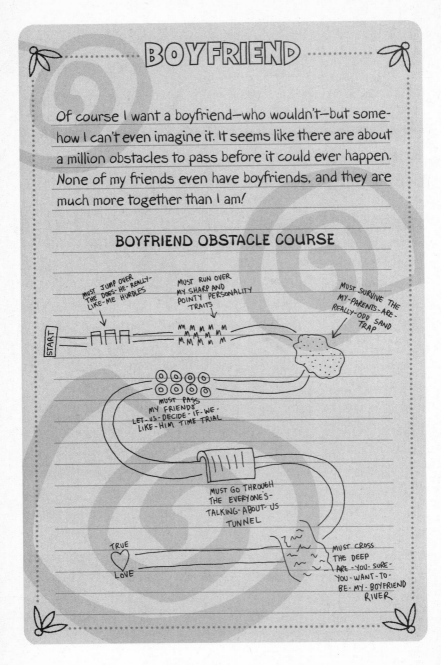

MUST JUMP OVER
THE DOES-HE-REALLY-
LIKE-ME HURDLES

MUST RUN OVER
MY SHARP AND
POINTY PERSONALITY
TRAITS

MUST SURVIVE THE
MY-PARENTS-ARE-
REALLY-ODD SAND
TRAP

START

MUST PASS
MY FRIENDS'
LET-US-DECIDE-IF-WE-
LIKE-HIM TIME TRIAL

MUST GO THROUGH
THE EVERYONE'S-
TALKING-ABOUT-US
TUNNEL

TRUE
LOVE

MUST CROSS
THE DEEP
ARE-YOU-SURE-
YOU-WANT-TO-
BE-MY-BOYFRIEND
RIVER

i got to dance with Andrew in dance class today. He asked about the new bruise on my leg (I wish we didn't have to wear our stupid shorts). I tried to be funny and told him about falling off my bike on Sunday. He didn't laugh out loud, but he was SMILING AT ME. He has a great smile! We had a great class and it totally made up for having to play basketball for the last half hour.

On the way out of the locker room, I overheard nosy Janelle ask Kathy, "What's the deal with Andrew and Emily? They aren't going out are they?" I pretended not to hear her, but it was a little weird. Good or bad weird, I'm not sure. It's strange to have people you don't like or even know talk about you. I wanted to tell Sandra all about the class—how perfect it felt to be dancing with Andrew even if we didn't know what we were doing, how funny and interesting he was, how he made me feel nervous in a good way—but I didn't. Sandra was still not being like her normal self, like she's unhappy about something. You shouldn't go on and on about how great your life is when your best friend is feeling kind of crummy, so we just talked about my library interview instead. Sandra said I shouldn't act too enthusiastic and perky because people in libraries are drowsy and slow—kind of like they just woke up fifteen minutes ago, and perky can be annoying if you are sleepy.

The whole thing was making me nervous . . . not because I was so desperate to get the job but more because it was like a test—a test I couldn't study for. Plus, I wasn't sure if they'd know about the four overdue library books in my room—almost a whole year overdue! I ended up picking my own outfit since Sandra was too preoccupied to help. I decided to wear my normal clothes (but not jeans—you're not allowed to wear jeans if you work at the library) and not worry about trying to look the part. Mom offered to buy me special work clothes if I got the job—probably ugly stuff I couldn't wear anywhere else.

I was excited on the bus ride down there, feeling more grown-up and together than usual. The lady at the front desk was not very friendly and had me wait until some other not-so-friendly lady came to get me. It was pretty uncomfortable just standing there. She was reading some kind of fashion magazine and just before unfriendly lady number two arrived, I caught a glimpse of Sandra's new black shirt in a section called MUST-HAVES. I couldn't tell what magazine it was, but it looked like a good one.

I followed the lady down to the basement. It was creepy—like, if it were a movie scene you'd shout, "Don't go down there!" if you were watching a scary movie. The interview lady (lady number three—there didn't seem to be very many guys working there), Ms. Dempster, was surprisingly cheerful and kept apologizing for how messy her office was. There were stacks of books and papers everywhere. She seemed more nervous than I was and kept moving around the room, like one of those birds you see in the pet-store cages that can't decide where to sit.

OOH. WHERE SHOULD I GO NEXT?

BIRD SITS HERE THEN THERE AND THERE AND THERE...

It was kind of funny to be interviewing for a job that involved organizing books in such a disorganized place. I thought they might give me an alphabet test or something, but Ms. Dempster just asked me if I knew the Dewey decimal system. Then she asked me some questions about my skills: what I thought I was good at, why I wanted to work at the library, what I liked about my past jobs. Pretty normal stuff. She asked me what skills I wanted to improve upon. In real life, there's a list of about a million things, but you can't just say the truth in an interview. They want to hear stuff like "I'd like to try and be less of a perfectionist," or "I feel like my attention to detail sometimes slows me down." I just said I was looking forward to the challenge of working with new and different people. Ms. Dempster kind of rolled her eyes and said, "Well, there sure are some different people working here." I gave her my best oh-great-I-can't-wait-to-meet-them smile, which of course wasn't true. She was probably talking about Mrs. Wilson's son, Paul—he definitely fits in the different category. She said a couple more things about the job and then had me follow her back up to the main entrance and that was it. I'm glad it's over. Now I'm not even sure I'd like working there. It would be odd to spend all day in a place where you aren't allowed to talk.

I called Sandra as soon as I got home and told her about the interview and that I'd seen her new black shirt in the MUST-HAVE section of a fashion magazine. She was her old self again, which was very, very nice! What if everything worked out? I thought about asking about Claire again but chickened out. Maybe I was wrong anyway. Wouldn't be the first time my imagination got out of control.

BOYFRIEND? + JOB? = VERY SURPRISED EMILY

Chapter 23

WeDNesDAY

UNBELIEVABLE

That the same person can be hit by lightning more than once.

That my parents, who yesterday seemed to only tolerate each other are now madly in love for no apparent reason.

That someone way back when decided to eat some of that gross stuff people eat.

That I am related to a caveman.

That someone who you know is your friend can hurt you on so many levels.

That something as disgusting as liver can actually be good for you to eat.

That I could be standing upside down on the earth right this minute and not even know it.

That people who have known me since I was born do not really know me.

That saying every cloud has a silver lining is supposed to make you feel better.

That some people try so hard and fail and others don't try at all and succeed.

That life never seems to be fair. Why do we even have that word?

i don't even know where to start. I feel like I've been hit by one of those eighteen-wheel delivery trucks except that for once all my bruises are on the inside, so nobody can tell but me! I was standing at my locker at lunchtime, waiting for Sandra and just chatting with Mike. In fact, I was kind of annoyed with him because now he's always hanging around when Sandra shows up, like he wants to be best buddies with us or something. WELL, BIG SURPRISE! Anyway, when Sandra got there she grabbed my arm and dragged me downstairs saying, "We have to talk." Then she started fumbling around saying stuff like, "I don't know how to tell you this," "This is so uncomfortable," and "I should have told you this before." Of course I was going nuts trying to think of what she was going to say. But then I remembered about Claire, so I totally knew what was wrong.

I couldn't wait for her to finish and blurted out, "I'm so sorry she got pregnant! Are your parents going to send her away?"

Sandra seemed confused, "Pregnant? Who's pregnant? Send who away?"

"Claire's pregnant, isn't she?" Now I was confused.

"Claire's not pregnant. This is about me. I'm dating Mike."

I was still confused. "Mike? Mike who?"

Sandra let out a big sigh and said, "Mike. You know Mike. Mike-by-your-locker Mike." Then she looked at me like she thought my head was going to explode, which it did, but she couldn't tell because it was an internal explosion—a nuclear meltdown!

"MIKE! YOU'RE DATING MIKE! But he's so short!" Looking back on it, the short comment was a stupid I'm-in-shock thing to say.

I guess Sandra thought so, too, because she just said, "He's not so short—he's as tall as you," and then kept repeating how sorry she was. It was one of those things where I had a million and one questions but no real way to express myself since I suddenly couldn't speak. All I could do was make a couple of weird sounds while trying to say how, when, and why, all at the same time. Sandra must have taken this as "So tell me about it," because she gave me a quick how-it-all-happened outline.

HOW IT ALL HAPPENED (according to Sandra)
Or
MY ADVENTURES BEHIND MY BEST FRIEND'S BACK
(my subtitle)

- She started to talk to him after I got mad at him for not telling me about the size label on my pants.
- She talked to him some more when I wasn't responding to his notes in my locker because he was upset and confused.
- She thought he was sweet because he seemed so concerned about me. She started to get a crush on him but thought that nothing would ever happen.
- One day they just bumped into each other at the drug store and ended up talking for almost two hours.
- He started to put funny notes in HER locker.
- Sandra gave him her phone number on one of the notes she sent back.
- They started talking on the phone at night.
- They met a couple of times at the playground in the park.
- On Saturday he kissed her, and now they are going out. DATING!!!

THIS WHOLE THING IS JUST SO
"I CAN'T BELIEVE IT!!!!"

Sandra was such a mess of worry and nervousness, and I was such a mess of confusion and I don't know what else that we decided to wait until after school to talk about it some more. I was almost halfway back to my locker to get my books when I realized that Mike (SANDRA'S BOYFRIEND) might be there. I waited in the girl's changing room until the buzzer rang before grabbing all my stuff for the rest of the afternoon—I even took my coat. I was not going back there! The rest of the day was a blur of normal school stuff, which couldn't end fast enough. I must have been the first one out of the building when the final buzzer rang. All the way home, I imagined Mike and Sandra talking at my locker.

MIKE: Did you tell her?

SANDRA: Yeah, she was upset.

MIKE: Really upset or just kind of upset?

SANDRA: Really upset. She couldn't even talk.

MIKE: How much did you tell her?

SANDRA: Just a short of outline of what happened.

MIKE: Did she say anything about me?

SANDRA: No, she didn't say anything about anything. She's supposed to meet me here.

MIKE: Maybe I should go.

SANDRA: Oh, don't go! I'll miss you.

MIKE: You're right, we're together now. She'll just have to get used to it.

SANDRA: Oh, she will. Everything is going to be perfect!

By the time I walked in the front door, I felt like I was going to throw up. Really!

After about an hour I started making a list of questions for Sandra—something to sort out the jumbled disaster mess that was spinning around in my head—at about a million miles an hour. I e-mailed it to her, which we never do, because I hate going into my basement and we decided eons ago that e-mails are too impersonal. Tonight impersonal sounded perfect. It was a lot easier to write it down than it would have been to say it. The only bad part was that I had to phone her to tell her that I'd sent her an e-mail, but I hung up before she could say anything back. After about two hours of trying not to think about it, one spent with Mom and Dad being their now weirdly cheery selves at dinner, I went downstairs to check the computer. Sandra had answered all my questions. . . .

QUESTIONS FOR SANDRA TO HELP EMILY UNDER-STAND WHAT HAPPENED AND WHY!

1. Why didn't you tell me about Mike way back when you had a crush on him?

I didn't tell you anything because I was sure he didn't like me; in fact, I always figured he had kind of a crush on you. I didn't want you to feel like I was hanging around your locker just so I could be close to Mike— even though in the end a little bit of that happened. It just seemed too awkward and, besides, you wanted me to like Jason. I guess I just thought I would get over it. I didn't like him on purpose—it just happened.

2. How could you keep this a secret from me when I was telling you absolutely everything about Andrew?

At first when I was talking to Mike we were talking about you. I think he kind of felt you didn't want to be his friend anymore, and I just wanted to try and smooth things over. I thought you would be mad at me for talking about you behind your back. I was only doing it because I wanted you two to stay friends. I should have told you from the start that I was talking to him, but I just thought he and I would have a chat or two and then it would all be resolved. When things got more serious with Mike, things were not going so well with you and Andrew. I felt uncomfortable telling you how great my guy-relationship life was when yours wasn't turning out like you wanted. I guess I was a coward. It was wrong! You're my best friend, and even though you may not believe me, it was really hard not to share that with you. I even wrote you a couple of letters explaining everything but chickened out before I could give them to you. I did and do feel terrible!

3. Didn't you feel like you were cheating on our friendship?

At first I felt like I was saving you from being upset . . . but then I started feeling guilty and uncomfortable whenever we were together—so I guess I did.

4. When you said you had to do all that stuff with Claire, were you actually meeting Mike?

Yes, kind of. I'm sorry I lied. I've been a horrible friend!

5. Did you tell him personal stuff about me? Anything about Andrew?

I swear I did not tell him anything about Andrew or anything personal about you except what a great friend and fantastic person you are—I think he already knew that anyway.

6. How are we supposed to be best friends after this?

I don't know. I guess I'll have to prove to you that you can still trust me—that I am worth forgiving.

7. Is Mike your new best friend?

No! You are my best friend.

Here are some words that describe how I'm feeling:

LOSERISH	FOOLISH	LEFT OUT
BETRAYED	DUMPED	SAD
LONELY	SICK	MAD
	SHOCKED	

I am so sorry that I made you feel that way!

I feel sick!!! I'm going to be sick. Please! Please! Please! Forgive me!

I reread Sandra's answers about 500 times. I believed her, but I couldn't decide what to think about us. I'm her best friend, and she kept this huge secret from me. And she lied to keep me from finding out. There I was thinking, Poor Sandra, she's got to spend so much time with Claire. And then I was worried that Claire was pregnant when all along Sandra was laughing and having a great time with Mike. Good thing I was a chicken and didn't confront Claire for being so needy. I would have looked like a complete idiot! Plus, Mike was in on it—like it was them against me! Plus, he's her boyfriend!!! Not a guy she just likes, but a boyfriend!!! Where was the whole crush lead-up!? We like each other, we kiss, we're going out. Nobody gets a boyfriend that fast—it's like a corny TV romance!

173

Tomorrow is going to be a hard day.

Chapter 24

THURSDAY

CONTROL
Things I Can't

It just seems that almost every part of my life just happens, and I don't have any power over what happens or when. I'm like a juggler who's standing in front of an audience and people keep throwing me stuff (apples, pumpkins, eggs, chainsaws), and I have to keep it all in the air. And I'm supposed to make it look like it's easy to do. It's impossible!!!

I wake up every morning, and I don't know if I should be wearing armor or a sundress.

And I mostly always pick wrong.

I wanted to stay home from school today—not sure I was ready to see MIKE or Sandra. It's totally my luck that his locker is next to mine. Could it be any more awkward? But today was Thursday, and my desire to see Andrew overruled any pretend illness, so I went. My plan was to avoid M and S at all costs—not even go to my locker, which meant that I had to carry around my jacket again. The first part of the morning went as planned. No M and S sightings, and I got to gym class without any trouble.

While we were changing, Janelle kept giving me looks like she wanted to say something but couldn't decide if she should or not. I pretended not to notice, but I could see her out of the corner of my eye—I'm pretty good at that. I really hate her.

When we went out to the gym, the guys were already there. Everyone started to pair up, but I couldn't find Andrew. He wasn't there! Finally, there was just me and two guys standing off to the side: One was a guy named Devon and the other was a guy I didn't know. Before I could figure out what to do, Ms. Clark paired me up with the guy I didn't know and took Devon as her partner. Devon seemed pretty happy, probably because Ms. Clark is so hot-looking. My partner said his name was Miles, and I was surprised that he already knew who I was. It was hard to concentrate because I kept trying to imagine what had happened to Andrew and Miles was Mr. Jibber-Jabber about everything. So between listening to him, worrying about Andrew, and trying to count dance steps, it was a total disaster.

In the changing room after class, Janelle came over to me and asked in a really loud voice, "So where's your boyfriend today?" Then she looked around to make sure everyone was paying attention, which they were. "He's not my boyfriend! And why would I ever tell you anything!" I was almost shouting at her. What I really wanted to say was, "I hate you! You nosy bitch!" But Janelle is the kind of person who could jump you and start pulling your hair, so I had to be careful.

She looked around the room and went, "OOOHHH, so touchy!" but people weren't paying attention anymore—I'm not the only one who thinks she's awful! I got dressed as fast as I could before she could think of something nasty to say. She's not very smart, so I was out the door before she had a chance to open her big fat mouth again. And then I walked home—right in the middle of third period.

Mom wasn't home, so I didn't have to face that obstacle. Of course, all I could think about was Sandra. In a way it was like being cheated on by a boyfriend or a husband, and I couldn't help but go back over the last few weeks looking for clues that I'd missed. That's the worst part of all this—feeling like it was right there in front of my eyes, but I was too stupid and wrapped up in my own little life to see it.

CHEATER CATEGORIES

KINDS OF CHEATERS	SANDRA
1. THOSE WHO ARE SUDDENLY SUPER NICE AND FRIENDLY TO THEIR SPOUSE TO TRY AND COVER UP THEIR CHEATING AND GUILT	
2. THOSE WHO ACT PERFECTLY NORMAL IN EVERY WAY	
3. THOSE WHO PULL AWAY AND ACT DISTANT BECAUSE THEY FEEL SO GUILTY	X

In a way it makes me feel a little better that Sandra is a category three. Somehow, knowing that she was suffering and not really good at it is sort of reassuring. It's not like I don't want to be friends with her anymore; it's just that I don't know what to do next. How to talk to her like everything is normal. How to act if we are together and suddenly Mike walks up. How to even say anything to him. I was thinking about all this when the doorbell rang. Sometimes it's nice to be interrupted if your mind is just going crazy.

As I was coming down the stairs, I could see that it was Sandra. I wanted to turn around and go hide in my room, but I knew that she'd seen me. It was weird standing at the door just looking at each other—best friends and not knowing what to say. Then Sandra handed me a bunch of flowers (my first bouquet) and followed me into the kitchen so I could put them in some water.

The next hour was pretty awful: lots of unhappy back and forth until we both ended up crying. Neither of us is a grudge keeper, so I knew in the end we'd get back to being best friends; I just didn't know how we'd get there. We made some lunch and spent the rest of the afternoon talking. At first I wasn't sure how much I wanted to know about her and Mike, and she was being careful to give out info only if I asked for it. But in the end I guess I'm pretty nosy, because I couldn't help but ask a lot of questions. She was really excited about him, which was a little hard to get used to since we were just talking about the same old Mike. I started to feel kind of uncomfortable when she started talking about their first kiss. She said it was the best kiss she'd ever had. She said that Mike had said it was his best kiss too.

"His best kiss too? Really? Did he tell you about his others?" I asked.

"No! He's not that kind of guy." I suppose she was kind of offended that I seemed surprised that she had given Mike his best kiss ever. I tried to make up for it by asking for more details.

"Where did it happen?"

"At the tire swing."

"Were you surprised?"

"No, I knew it was going to happen. I could just feel it."

"Was it weird afterward?"

"No! It was great!"

Stuff like that.

I'm happy for her, really! It's just weird hearing all about her

EVOLUTION OF MY HAPPY FACE

love life when I'm the one who's been talking about a guy for the last couple of weeks. By the time Sandra left, I'm sure she was feeling better. I'm not sure how much better I was feeling. I think it's harder to be the one who was cheated on.

IF CHEATING WERE A SOLID THING
(WHICH IS HARDER?)

PILLOW
(THE ONE WHO
CHEATED)

BOULDER
(THE ONE WHO
WAS CHEATED ON)

Mom arrived home a little after that and made a big deal about the flowers. At first she thought they were for her from Dad, and then when I said they were mine she got all nosy like she thought they were from a boy. (I guess nosy runs in the family.) I must have still been upset because I told her the whole Sandra-Mike story, which normally I never would have done. She was a perfect mom and said all the right things. Not stuff like, "Sandra is a horrible friend," but more like how she could see that my feelings would be hurt and how it seemed perfectly understandable that the whole thing would make me feel awkward. She said she always thought the lead-up to a romance could be as exciting and important as the romance itself. Sandra ripped me off! I didn't get to be part of her lead-up! It's weird how when some things are going just awful, other things surprise you by unexpectedly going right. For the first time ever, I thought that if Mom were my age and we were in school together, maybe I would like her.

LATER

We had a nice, normal dinner.

EVEN LATER

Before bed I promised myself: I will be brave and face Mike tomorrow! I will be nice and not freak out!

I will be normal—but in a good way!

I was so wrapped up in Sandra and Mike, I forgot all about Andrew. I wonder where he was today!

Chapter 25

FRIDAY

DENIAL

THE KISS

Question

If something happens and everyone who was there when it happened acts like it didn't, then can't you forget about it and stop worrying that you'll be found out because it sort of never really happened?

Answer: No

KISS

Mistake + Kiss = Kisstake

I'll probably forget all about it since I've been trying so hard to pretend it never happened. So maybe it's good that I'm writing it down. A while ago, way before he and Sandra hooked up, Mike called me and asked me to meet him at the park. I should have said, "No, I'm busy" or something because I knew he liked me. But I didn't want to be mean, so I was chicken and said sure. He wanted to sit on the tire swing together and just talk. Normally, I like talking to Mike, but I was really nervous and uncomfortable. We talked for a while and then he started to kiss me. I knew it was coming, but I did nothing to stop it. It was an okay kiss, but as soon as it was over and I was looking at him, I wished it never happened. He looked like he was waiting for me to smile or say something, but I couldn't think of anything. We sat there for about three or four minutes not talking, and then I said I had to go. The whole thing was wrong. We never talked about it, and I'm pretty sure he didn't tell Sandra. I would just die if he told her. I feel pretty guilty, and I know I did a really bad job of handling it. I'm sure he hates me. What if he makes Sandra hate me too?

Just like me to be writing about a kiss that should not have happened instead of a great want-to-remember-it-forever kiss.

Facing Mike was like taking cough medicine: the worst part was the thinking-about-it part. I went straight to my locker and waited around until he showed up. Better to get the uncomfortable stuff over with as fast as possible. I could tell he was really nervous, because he was being serious and usually he's kind of jokey. I told him that I'd talked to Sandra, which he probably already knew since Sandra said they talk every night, and that I was glad that she'd found someone nice to be with. Of course it didn't come out that easily, but I think he got what I was trying to say. I guess he felt relieved because he started acting a little more like himself. It was still uncomfortable, though. I wanted to ask him if he was planning on telling Sandra about our kiss thing. I was so sure she'd be mad especially since:

1. I had kept it a secret AND
2. It had happened at the tire swing.

Would she think that her "special" kiss meant less?

	SANDRA	ME
BOY	Mike	Mike
PLACE	Tire Swing	Tire swing
RESULT	Excellent	Wrong

That Mike was unoriginal? But how do you bring up something like that? I couldn't do it. We were just chatting, pretending that

186

everything was the same, when Sandra arrived. I was so nervous I could hardly look at them. I don't know what I was expecting; it's not like they were going to start making out right there in the hallway. They just seemed really happy to see each other. Sandra promised to meet me at lunch and then the bell rang and it was back to normal—almost.

During band class, Sarah W. kept trying to tell me something, but I couldn't figure out what she was saying. She doesn't sit next to me so it's hard to hear even a loud whisper if there are five other people in the way. I was finally able to figure out that she was saying, "Why didn't you tell me?" After class she came running over and said, "How come you didn't tell me?" I couldn't believe that she knew about Sandra and Mike already. I told her I'd just found out myself. She looked confused and said, "Well that's not what Miles said. He said you and Andrew have been partners for weeks."

"Oh, that. I thought you were talking about something else." Luckily, she was so interested in the Andrew thing she didn't ask about the something else. I'm not sure she would have cared anyway since she's not a big Sandra fan. I said it was just a dumb dance class and it didn't mean anything. But Sarah W.'s not an idiot; she knew I was lying. She grabbed my arm in that best-friends way and pulled me to the side of the room. I thought she was mad, but instead she just smiled and said, "Do you have dance class today? I want you to give Andrew a message about the sleepover."

"Is Andrew coming to the sleepover?" Sarah rolled her eyes like I was the stupidest person on the planet.

"No! Are you crazy? Do you have class today or not?" When I said no she completely lost interest in talking to me and said, "I'll just do it myself." I looked at Sarah J. for help, but all she would say was, "It's a surprise." What am I supposed to do with this information?

SLEEPOVER ANDREW SURPRISE

It's like everyone I know is purposefully trying to make me lose my mind!

I had lunch with Sandra (I thought she might invite Mike, but she didn't) and told her about the sleepover intrigue. She shook her head and said Sarah W.'s brain was a strange and scary place. Easy for her to say! Apart from that, she seemed pretty excited about Saturday night. In fact, she was in a great mood. I've never slept at someone else's house, not including Sandra's house or one belonging to a relative, and Sarah W.'s parents are really rich so it's probably a really great place. Before lunch ended, Sandra said she had no idea what the Andrew surprise thing was going to be but that she'd be there with me so not to worry. It was nice of her, and it made me feel a little better . . . but I'm still worried!

We all walked home together—Sandra, Mike, and me. Sandra and Mike held hands, which was weird. Every time I looked at their hands, my ears started to get hot and red.

DON'T LOOK RULE

Once you decide to try and ignore something and not look at it, it's almost impossible to keep your eyes from going there accidentally.

When we were almost home, Mike said he had to turn off and he gave Sandra's hand a little extra squeeze. They probably would have kissed if I wasn't there, but Sandra didn't seem disappointed. I'm sure she wanted to talk about him and say things like:

"Isn't he cute?"

"He's got the greatest hands."

"He gave me a special good-bye squeeze. Did you see it?"

But she didn't because she knows I'm just getting used to them being a "them." She really is trying.

When I got home there was a message from the library. I GOT THE JOB! I can't believe it! I start next Saturday in the fine art department. Mom said we had to go out to celebrate. We had a great sushi dinner. Dad tried to be all macho and eat something with a raw egg on it but ended up spitting it into his napkin (gross). It was pretty funny!

More handholding on the way home—theme for the day? But this time it didn't bother me as much. I hope I get that way with Sandra and Mike too.

It's impossible to force yourself not to think about something that's bugging you. I'll probably have horrible Andrew surprise dreams all night!

Chapter 26

SATURDAY
SUNDAY

MOVIES

I love movies! I love everything about them—the popcorn, the previews, and

FOR THE NEXT HOUR I AM GOING TO LAUGH, THEN CRY, THEN LAUGH AGAIN!

even the people in the audience. I like it when there's some guy who can't stop laughing at the funny part and then pretty soon everyone is laughing at the guy. I like checking off the previews into "gotta see that" and "that looks terrible" categories. I like the way the music lets you know what is about to happen so you can be prepared—scary music when something bad is going to happen and happy music when you don't have to worry. It doesn't spoil it. It's like a roller coaster: The ride isn't ruined when you are going up a hill and know that the downhill is next, you're just more prepared is all. I love crying at the sad parts and then hearing the person behind me sniffling too. I love how the whole story will be wrapped up in under two hours so you don't have to think about it after that if you don't want to. I love getting to decide what I want to see and when, so that if you want to laugh you go to a comedy and if you want excitement you go to an action film. I love how movies give me the power over my emotions! I get to be the boss!

Spent most of the day just hanging around the house not doing anything exciting and waiting until it was time to pick up Sandra and go to Sarah W.'s house. Before we left, Sandra and I spent about an hour on the phone trying to figure out which pajamas to bring: cute nightie or regular pajamas.

CUTE NIGHTIE   PJ's

We decided to take them both and choose once we got there. I was surprised how nervous I was. Mom drove through the entrance gate and right to the door. I was hoping she'd just drop us off on the street. She turned the car off like she was going to come in too so we jumped out, said good-bye, and slammed the door before she could do anything like follow us. Sarah's mom let us in and waved good-bye to Mom so she had no choice but to drive off. I'm sure Mom wanted to see the inside of the house.

Sarah's mom was all dressed up and said she was going out and that Sarah was in the kitchen. Sarah's kitchen was huge! As soon as she saw us, Sarah J. came over and gave us big hugs like she'd been waiting forever for us to get there. There was no sign of Andrew. We had a great dinner of shrimp cocktail, pizza, and some kind of fancy drink that looked alcoholic but wasn't—it had an umbrella in it.

After dinner we watched a couple of movies and ate more food. Sarah has a huge TV—it was almost like being in a movie theater, except her seats were more comfy. Sandra and Sarah W. were even acting like they almost liked each other. At about 1:30 A.M., Sarah announced that it was time for bed. It seemed a little bossy since everyone was having such a good time and didn't seem at all tired. I was disappointed that we weren't going to sleep in her room—she said it was too small. It's hard to consider someone your friend if you've never even seen her bedroom. The den was all set up with mattresses on the floor. I asked if we could watch the small (but still pretty big) TV, which was in the den, until we fell asleep, but Sarah said no because we had to get up really early for the surprise. And then she and Sarah J. started giggling about their big secret. It was really uncomfortable and rude! Sandra sort of told them off and they apologized, but I was still upset. If I hadn't been so full, I'm sure I would have had a hard time falling asleep. The next thing I knew, Sarah W. was shaking me and saying it was time to wake up. At first I thought something bad had happened because it was still dark outside, but she said everything was fine, it was just time for the surprise. We had to put on our coats and shoes before she told us what was going on. I was glad that we were wearing pajamas and not our nighties since we were obviously going outside. She gave us all a mug of hot chocolate—very organized—and then said we were going to walk to Andrew's house for a pre-breakfast breakfast because he was having a slumber party too. Right away I could tell that Sandra didn't think this was a very good idea, and I wasn't sure how much I wanted to see Andrew and Sarah W. being all chummy chummy. But Sarah is one of those people who ALWAYS gets what she wants, so off we went. She said we'd be back way before her mom got up, so no one would even know we were gone.

Once we got going, it was pretty fun and exciting. The sun was just coming up, and there was absolutely no one around. Sarah said she knew the best way to get to Andrew's house, which made it seem like she had probably been there before.

Here's the really weird part. We were just walking along King Street, which is kind of busy, when a car starts honking at us. "Just some weirdos," said Sarah W., "ignore them." But the car slowed down like it was following us and didn't stop honking.

"EEEWWW . . . it's a bunch of old guys," whispered Sarah J., "don't look at them." Of course, when someone says don't look you have to take a peek. Sandra and I both looked at the same time.

"OH NO, IT'S MY DAD!" screamed Sandra and then she covered her mouth like she might be sick or something. Now we all looked at the car! Sandra's dad was smiling and waving like crazy, so we all gave a little wave back. He beeped the horn twice and then drove away towing *Suzanne* (his boat) behind him. "He's going fishing," said Sandra.

"Will he tell your mom?" asked Sarah J.

"Maybe, maybe not," said Sandra, "he forgets a lot of normal stuff."

"That's the good thing about dads," I said, and everyone shook their heads.

"Yeah, he'll probably forget," mumbled Sandra.

"THAT WAS WEIRD!" said Sarah W. suddenly, like it had taken her that long to figure out what had happened, and we all started laughing and couldn't stop for almost two blocks. "It's the next block," said Sarah W. pointing, and my stomach started to get all nervous. Sandra held my hand, which she never does, and that made me feel a little braver. Longest block of my life or shortest block of my life—it was hard to decide. Sarah W. started getting excited and talking about some guy named Marco. By the time we got to Andrew's house, it was obvious that Marco was Andrew's best friend and that Sarah W. had a huge crush on him. I gave Sandra's hand an I-can't-believe-everything-is-going-to-be-okay squeeze. She squeezed back a you-betcha. It was weird to see Andrew so early in the morning and while I was still dressed in my pajamas. I introduced him to Sandra and he offered her a donut from a box—our pre-breakfast breakfast. Marco was soap opera handsome—no wonder Sarah W. liked him. Andrew, Sandra, Sarah J., and I all sat on the front steps eating donuts for about half an hour. Andrew was really nice and included everyone in the conversation. Sarah W. and Marco disappeared a couple of minutes after we got there. They were probably making out somewhere.

Andrew said he had both an older sister and a younger brother. So he and Sandra talked about older sisters and he and Sarah J. talked about younger brothers. I didn't even know that Sarah J. had a younger brother. Then they all said they felt bad for me because I didn't have any siblings. That was kind of uncomfortable. I said, "Well, I get everything for myself that way. The channel clicker, the crusty end of the bread, and all the toys! I don't have to share." Andrew and Sarah J. thought that was pretty funny and laughed.

But then Sandra said, "But you don't have anyone you can really yell at and be mean to who you know has to forgive you and still love you when it's all over. You can't treat a friend like you treat a sibling! They just wouldn't stand for it." Both Sarah J. and Andrew nodded.

Then Andrew said, "Yeah, you're really missing out Ems (it was so weird that he called me that!). My little brother called me a poopy-head the other day, and it was so special!" Everybody laughed and then we talked about stuff that I knew something about: school, Sandra's dad seeing us, and snoring. Andrew said his friend Marco is a real snorer—nice to know nobody's perfect. Then before I knew it, Sarah W. and Marco were back, and Sarah W. said it was time to go. She sure likes being the boss of the party!

Andrew said a general good-bye to everyone and then said, "I'll see YOU on Tuesday" to me. YIPPEE!!!!—something I'm writing but would never say, because it sounds too lame. All the way home Sarah W. only wanted to talk about Marco and how fabulous he was at this and that. Poor Sarah J., Sandra and I walked a little behind, so we didn't have to participate in the Marco fest. Sandra said that she thought Andrew was sweet, and I could tell that she meant it and wasn't just saying something nice to make me feel good. We got back to Sarah W.'s house at about 7:15. I was exhausted. We snuck back into the den and just crashed. As I was falling asleep I was thinking that we all had someone except Sarah J. I should try and be extra nice to Sarah J.

Sarah W.'s mom woke us up at about 10 A.M. She said she was making pancakes and scrambled eggs in the kitchen. I was still full from dinner and the donuts but forced down a pancake. I think she was disappointed that we all seemed so tired. Sandra was right (about the library): Perky is really annoying when you are sleepy.

After breakfast, Sarah W. started up about Marco again so Sandra and I decided to leave. I gave both the Sarahs a hug good-bye and thanked them for the surprise. "It was worth the wait, wasn't it?" said Sarah W., and I smiled a non-pretend smile and said, "Yes." Sometimes she seems so perfect.

We walked to Sandra's house and just napped most of the afternoon. Surprisingly, Sandra had a few nice things to say about Sarah W. There might be friendship hope for them after all. I called Mom to come get me at around dinnertime. She was surprised and disappointed that I wasn't still at Sarah W.'s. I promised to give her a full description of the house on the way home. I couldn't eat any dinner so I went upstairs to rest and reevaluate my spinning world.

WHAT I NOW KNOW ABOUT ANDREW

The name of his best friend is not James, but Marco.
He has a brother named Jackson who is six years old.
He likes plain cake donuts the best and doesn't like chocolate frosted ones.
He looks super cute with his hair messed up from sleeping.
He lives in a nice, normal-looking house.
He does NOT have a crush on Sarah W.

Thank you, Sarah W.

Chapter 27

MONDAY

HAPPINESS

Mom seems happier lately. While we were doing dishes the other day I said something about it. At first she seemed surprised that I had noticed. I didn't say anything about her being jealous of me but said that Dad had told me he had been worried about her. Mom smiled and said that sometimes Dad thought he knew what was going on but he really didn't have a clue, but that she was glad that he was trying. I asked if it had anything to do with desserts. She laughed and said that not all problems can be solved with a box of donuts. It was kind of confusing, but I think that Mom was just happy that Dad was paying more attention to her. She'll probably get grumpy again when Dad figures she is fine and stops. Or maybe not—maybe this time the happiness will stick. That's all you can really hope for—super glue-strength happiness.

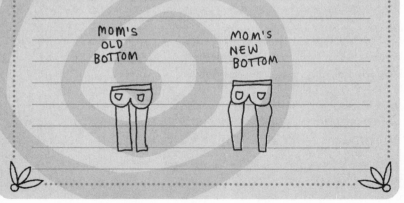

MOM'S OLD BOTTOM

MOM'S NEW BOTTOM

i was still sleepy today. I had lunch with the Sarahs (decided to give Sandra and Mike a little private time). Of course we talked about the slumber party and the trip to Andrew's house. Sarah W. is acting like she changed her mind and now thinks that Andrew might like me. It's like I'm suddenly more important. She even said that the four of us should do something sometime. I felt bad for Sarah J. because she meant Marco, Andrew, her, and me. Sarah J. just pretended like she didn't hear what we were talking about and rummaged in her bag like she was looking for something. I wondered if she still had that huge crush on David but couldn't figure out how to ask her about it. I didn't want her to get upset. It's hard to be in the Lonely Hearts Club all by yourself.

I tried to change the subject, but it's hard to get Sarah W. to do something she doesn't want to do. I'm sure Sarah J. had a miserable time all during lunch. It made me feel a little guilty to be so happy and chummy with Sarah W., like I was stealing Sarah J.'s best friend right in front of her. As we were cleaning up, I told Sarah J. that I was practicing my clarinet more and hoped that sometime soon I'd get good enough to move up to second clarinet and then we could sit together. She got really excited and said she'd even help me practice. I told her I didn't think I was good enough to play with her yet, but I'd let her know as soon as I was ready. Of course it was a total lie. I haven't been practicing at all, but I had to do something to make her feel better. And it's just an early lie, because I'm really

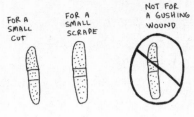

FOR A SMALL CUT

FOR A SMALL SCRAPE

NOT FOR A GUSHING WOUND

going to try and do it! Sometimes a little lie is okay if it doesn't hurt anyone and helps fix something. It's like a bandage.

Sandra and I walked home from school. Mike wasn't with us. Sandra said he had to go somewhere. It felt pre-Mike. She said her dad still hadn't said anything about seeing us when he was going on his fishing trip. We agreed that enough time had passed and that she was probably safe. It really is pretty funny when you think about it. Sandra asked if I was still excited about Andrew, which I was, and I asked if she was still excited about Mike, which she was. It was nice to both have guys to talk about. Sandra reminded me that we are going to get our French comic project back tomorrow. She's sure we are going to get an A—I hope she's right. I didn't do so great on the last test; an A would really help. Just before I turned off for my house, Sandra asked me not to say anything about her and Mike to Becca. She said she wanted to tell her herself, probably tomorrow. I said sure, it really wasn't my story to tell anyway. I could tell that she was nervous again.

SANDRA + MIKE

It's not easy to come clean after you have been lying. And keeping things from your friends is the same as lying, isn't it? I think the Sandra and Mike thing might be okay. I think I could get used to it.

Chapter 28

Tuesday

ANGER

I'M SO SICK AND MAD AT ANDREW
AND ME
THAT I CAN HARDLY WRITE ANYTHING!!!!!!

I'd love to be one of those cartoon characters on TV—
just for an hour—so that I could go around and just
smash stuff to bits with a giant sledgehammer.

That's IT! I GIVE UP! I'M SICK, SICK, SICK AND TIRED OF ALL THIS YES, NO, YES, NO, YES, NO!!!!

Everything was going fine today until I got to gym class. I gave Janelle the evil eye, hoping she'd keep her mouth shut, which she did. Andrew was there so we partnered up as usual and were having a nice chat. I even told him all about my new library job, until he noticed a bruise on my arm. I don't even know how I got it—probably bumped into something at home. Anyway, I brushed it off like it was nothing important, which it wasn't, but he kept on about it. Then out of the blue he asked me if I had a good relationship with my parents? Did they ever try to hurt me? I completely stopped moving. I must have looked absolutely shocked because he tried to cover up what he had said by saying, "I was only joking." But you don't joke about stuff like that. Ms. Clarke came over and asked if there was a problem because we were just standing in the middle of the floor, me with my mouth open and no sounds coming out. Andrew said, "No, we were just taking a break," and grabbed my hands.

After a couple of minutes of uncomfortable silent dancing I said, "Listen, I just bruise easily, and I'm kind of clumsy. That's it." It was like I had given Andrew the answer he wanted and now he was relieved and happy, but I was completely mortified! He was in a good mood the rest of the class and chatted happily away even though I was hardly talking back.

Right before class ended, he announced, "I'm going to call you Bruisy," like he was naming a pet or something. Then, as I was walking into the changing room, he called out, "See you Thursday, Bruisy." I didn't even answer back. I could hardly wait until lunchtime to tell Sandra about the disastrous crash of my super-brief love life. Sandra couldn't understand why I was so mad, and even when I explained it to her, I got the feeling she thought I was overreacting.

WHY I'M MAD

Andrew tricked me! He tricked me into liking him when all he wanted to do was save some poor, pitiful girl from her evil, abusive parents. It was a complete guy superhero-ego thing! Nobody names someone they want to date Bruisy! It's a hamster or a mean dog name!

Sandra seemed to think it was kind of cute that Andrew was so worried about me, but I just think the whole thing is sickening! Plus, I feel really stupid . . . for liking him, for flirting with him, for telling other people I thought something was going on, for everything! WHAT A BIG, DISGUSTING DISASTER!!!

When I got home I ripped up the little piece of paper from under my pillow, but it was too small to be very satisfying. I finally just punched the pillow a couple of times and lay on the bed until I got bored. Can true love turn to hate in just a few minutes? Maybe I never really liked him. Maybe I just wanted to like him so I thought I did. Maybe I just wanted someone to like me.

LATER

Sandra called to see how I was. I said I was A-OK. She seemed surprised by my answer, but I didn't really want to chat. What was there to say? So we had another record-breaking short call.

Really, I'm more mad at myself than I am at Andrew. He's just a stupid guy!

Chapter 29

WeDNesDAY

INVENTION

Reinvention

You can decide that you don't like something about yourself, but can you really change things? Can you wake up one morning and say, "From now on I'm going to be more confident" and then do it? Or do you just have to live with a whole list of things that you don't really like about yourself? It seems that almost every day my list is getting longer and longer. This is most definitely more of a girl than a guy problem. Actually really more of a woman problem, which is worse. It means it's something I'm not going to outgrow—so it's not going to get any better. That's why they have so many of those self-help, feel-good-type shows on TV during the day. Sad housewives across the country wish they were someone else. And I don't think it helps to know that there are others like you. It just seems more inevitable that you will end up joining the club you don't want to belong to.

I'm surprised with how okay I am with this whole Andrew thing. I don't even want to think about it. I guess the good thing is that now I can pal around with Sarah J.: two lonely hearts just hanging out. But I don't feel that lonely. Just strangely relieved, like maybe one of the major sources of the craziness in my life is now over.

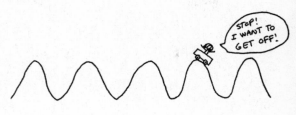

You can't ride the roller coaster forever.

School was okay. I had lunch with Sandra and Mike. They both like disgusting meat sandwiches, so they have more in common than I thought. They didn't hold hands or anything while they were eating, so no one but me knew that they are dating. It's kind of nice to be in on a secret. I'm now wondering if maybe Sandra's approach to love is best: Keep it to yourself until you know for sure that something is happening. I'll have to remember that for next time, if there is one. We finally got our French comic project back. We were supposed to get it yesterday, but Mademoiselle Swanson forgot them at home. We got an A just like Sandra said we would. Only two other people got As, so it meant a lot.

When I got home I practiced the clarinet for almost ninety minutes. My mouth was so sore I could hardly move it. I think it's going to take a lot of practice before I get any better. Mostly it's discouraging because when I play by myself it's so obvious how bad I am. It's easier to fool yourself into thinking you are pretty good when the whole band is playing. I'm sure Sarah J. would be shocked if she heard me play. She'd probably throw up. I think

I'm doing so well because I only lost something that I never really had in the first place. It's a lost fantasy.

Sandra told Becca about Mike today. Becca is so cool! She acted surprised, but she later told me that she knew something was up. I guess she saw Mike walking into the park that day she saw Sandra on the swings. Nobody ever tells me anything. I've got to start paying closer attention to what's going on around me! I'm like one of those carriage-pulling horses with the blinders on their eyes, only looking straight ahead.

ME WITH BLINDERS ON.
(CAN'T SEE OUT THE SIDE)

Chapter 30

THURSDAY

These are some things that I wish came in a bottle. Like a magic potion.

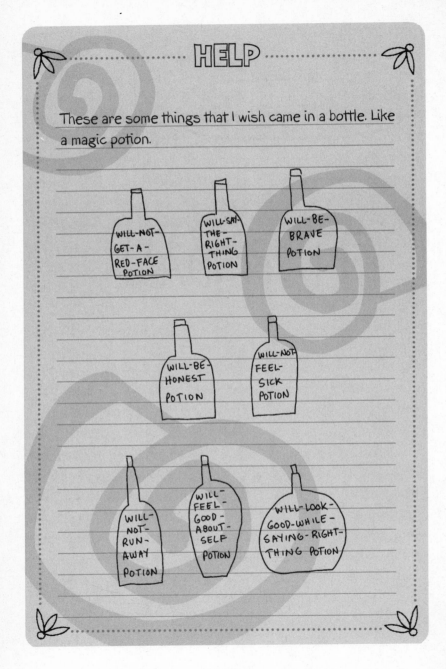

WILL-NOT-GET-A-RED-FACE POTION

WILL-SAY-THE-RIGHT-THING POTION

WILL-BE-BRAVE POTION

WILL-BE-HONEST POTION

WILL-NOT-FEEL-SICK POTION

WILL-NOT-RUN-AWAY POTION

WILL-FEEL-GOOD-ABOUT-SELF POTION

WILL-LOOK-GOOD-WHILE-SAYING-RIGHT-THING POTION

Today was the first test-date of the new me. I got to gym class a little bit early and dressed quickly so I'd be one of the first people into the gym. As soon as I saw Miles, I asked him to be my partner. I didn't even look to see if Andrew was there. Miles seemed surprised, but he didn't say no. I'm glad Miles likes to talk; it was easier to ignore what else might have be going on when I was busy chatting and counting steps. As soon as the class ended, I ran into the changing room. All in all, I was pretty pleased with my avoid-at-all-costs tactics.

At lunch Sarah J. asked me if I had been practicing my clarinet. It was nice to say yes and not be lying. Sarah W. didn't say anything about Marco or Andrew, which was totally not like her. She had probably spoken to Miles and knew something was up. It's so weird to have people talking about you behind your back. It makes you wonder, What do they know that they are not saying?

Becca decided to come over after school, so we walked home with Mike and Sandra. It was fun. Becca kept teasing them, telling them to give us a five-second warning if they were going to kiss, so we could look away. Mom and Dad were going out, so we decided to make banana pancakes for dinner. Sometimes it's fun to shake things up. Dad couldn't believe it; he's such a meat-for-supper kind of guy. He probably thought it was some kind of new fad—pancakes for dinner, what will they think of next? Mom was a little grumpy because she said her dress felt too tight across the butt. I said it looked fine, which it did, but she went upstairs and changed anyway. Is the happiness honeymoon going to be over? I hope not.

After dinner we watched a movie we had both seen before—no disappointments, no high expectations. We were completely satisfied. Mom and Dad got home at about 10 and then Mom and I drove Becca home. On the way back, Mom and I talked about her night out. She said that they had had a nice time except that the tables at the restaurant were too close together so she had trouble concentrating on what Dad was saying and kept trying to eavesdrop on the people next to them. She said Dad kept kicking her under the table, but she couldn't help it. She thought one of them might have been famous because he was talking about traveling and staying in hotels a lot, and the waiters all seemed to know who he was. I couldn't believe that she had had a celebrity sighting but didn't know who the celebrity was. Typical! She didn't seem to mind; she said it was still exciting. All in all not such a bad day, considering it could have been terrible. If I owned I'm-proud-of-me pajamas I'd have worn them!

Chapter 31

FRIDAY

MOVING
From Sadness

TIME TO GO!

Clouds of pain

Sometimes it's so hard to get up and go to school. It makes it a little more bearable if at least it's Friday. The entire day just dragged by . . . slow, slow, slow. I guess I was a little worried I'd bump into Andrew and he'd call me Bruisy—in a loud-enough-so-everyone-could-hear-it voice. But I didn't see him. What a horrible nickname. That's all I'd need to cement me into uncoolness forever. So what if I'm sensitive about my bruises? Who wouldn't be? If you had a big nose, you wouldn't want people to call you Nosy! At least I'll have the weekend to prepare my strategy for next week.

After school I came home and spent most of the evening trying to pick out something to wear to work tomorrow. I'm not allowed to wear jeans, sneakers, or T-shirts (they have a dress code for shelving books). I finally picked something out, but now my room is a complete disaster and I do not feel like cleaning it up.

LIBRARY OUTFIT FOR SATURDAY

SWEATER MOM BOUGHT FOR ME. I'VE ONLY WORN IT ONCE BEFORE BECAUSE SANDRA SAID, "THAT LOOKS LIKE A SWEATER YOUR MOM WOULD BUY." NOT A COMPLIMENT!

MY FAVORITE BLACK PANTS

BLACK SHOES. NOT GOOD FOR LOTS OF WALKING BUT THEY LOOK COOL.

I have to be there at 8:30, and it's a twenty-minute bus ride, so I have to get up even earlier than I do on a school day. It's a good thing they pay so well. Sandra said she wanted to come and see me at work in the afternoon, but I made her promise to wait until next week in case I was nervous and needed to concentrate.

I've been going over the alphabet in my head all day, like I might suddenly forget it if I don't practice. It's worse than having a song you don't like spinning around inside your brain. I asked Becca to meet me for lunch, but she was busy. I'm not excited about eating lunch all by myself in the library lunchroom. It's a real drag that Sandra doesn't get off work until 1:30! I'm getting nervous just thinking about all of this.

Chapter 32

SATURDAY

BELIEF

Some people believe that things will always turn out well, and others think they will always turn out badly.

I'm more on the "badly" side because then I won't be disappointed as much when things turn wrong. It's kind of a stupid way to operate because deep down I really do wish for good things.

What A DAY!!! I got to the library a little bit early and had to wait outside for them to open the main door. I didn't know there was a special employee entrance around the side. All this meant that I got to the Fine Art Department a little late. I thought they would be mad, but they were pretty nice about it. Work-wise my job is pretty easy. Someone in the basement puts all the books in order on little carts, a separate cart for each department. Then they send the carts up in a special cart elevator. I take them out of the elevator, shelve the books, and then send the empty carts back downstairs.

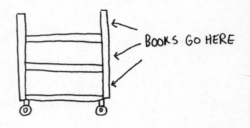

BOOKS GO HERE

The only other thing I have to do is listen for the librarian's bell. There's a whole special locked room behind the art department where they keep all the fancy books. When the librarian rings her bell, it means I have to go back there and find a book that a customer has asked for. It's a little stressful because the customer just waits at the librarian's desk so I feel as if I've really got to hurry. The first time I did this, I messed up and gave the book directly to the guy who was waiting. It seems stupid, but I'm supposed to hand it to the librarian and then she gives it to the customer. All in all I was doing okay until the librarian rang the bell about twenty minutes before lunch. I ran up to her desk and put my hand out for the key and the piece of paper with the book info, but she just said, "Someone to see you," and gave me a bit of a dirty look. I couldn't believe

I hadn't noticed him when I walked up to the desk, but there was Andrew standing right there!

"Let's talk," he said. I said I was working, but he said, "I'll just wait here until you're finished."

Then the librarian, Mrs. Fisher, interrupted and said, "Emily, perhaps it would be best if you met your friend downstairs in twenty minutes, when you have your lunch break."

Andrew seemed fine with that and said, "I'll see you downstairs," before I could even open my mouth to say, "But I don't want to talk to you!"

After Andrew left, Mrs. Fisher said that the library did not approve of "fraternizing with friends" during work hours. Then she smiled, patted my arm, and said, "Everyone makes a few mistakes on their first day." I knew my face was beet red because my ears were heating up like mini-volcanoes. It was impossible to concentrate. I think I only shelved five books in the twenty minutes before lunch.

There was no way to avoid Andrew since he was standing at the entrance waiting for me. When someone says, "Listen, I'm so sorry I hurt your feelings. I was stupid. Will you forgive me? Let's have lunch," you kind of have to have lunch with them. Andrew didn't have any lunch, so he ended up eating half of mine. I was too nervous to eat much anyway. I was just eating for show—acting like I was perfectly okay. He did most of the talking. The most important things he said were:

That he really liked me.
That he was sorry about the whole Bruisy thing and he never intended to hurt my feelings, and he would never call me that again.

That it was stupid to think that my parents were abusive.

That he liked being my partner in gym class.

That he wanted to meet me in the park tomorrow afternoon
    for a donut break at the swing.

After that we just talked about my job until it was time for me to go back to work. I was a smiling, happy worker all afternoon! The worse part was not being able to call Sandra to tell her what had happened. You're not allowed to use the library phone for private calls—even if you are on your break—and I didn't want to use the gross public phones.

After work I ran all the way to the bus stop, which was useless because I ended up waiting twenty-five minutes for my bus to get there. Mom wanted to hear all about my first day, but I told her I had to call Sandra first. Lucky day! Sandra was home. She said she was hysterically happy for me and invited me over for dinner. I went downstairs and told Mom all about the non-Andrew job things until she seemed satisfied and drove me to Sandra's.

When I got there, Sandra made me tell her the whole Andrew story again. At dinner she made a whisper toast to Mrs. Fisher, the grumpy matchmaker; we didn't want her whole family to hear it. She said she was sure that by the end of the day tomorrow I'd have a boyfriend too. I finally got her to stop talking about the boyfriend part—I didn't want to be disappointed if all I got was a donut. After that we talked about Mike and how she was going to break it to her parents about him. BRRRRRR . . . cold and scary thought. Even the coolest parents can be weird about boyfriends, and Sandra's parents aren't that cool. I think the whole Sandra-boyfriend thing is going to be okay. It definitely would have been harder to take if I didn't have someone who I liked too. I probably would have been jealous as well as hurt, and it's a lot harder to get over jealousy. It'll be different, that's for sure. Sandra let me borrow her new black shirt from the magazine and got her mom to drive me home. She said she was going to call Mike while her mom was gone (she has to be sneaky like that).

When I got home I tried on my meet-Andrew-at-the-park outfit. I'll have to wear my second favorite pair of jeans since my favorite ones are dirty. I still looked pretty good though.

LATER

Wrote Andrew's name on the fanciest piece of paper I could find and put it under my pillow.

Chapter 33

SUNDAY

i could hardly eat breakfast this morning; I was so nervous and excited. I hate how whenever you are waiting for something, the day just moves by so incredibly slowly—it almost seemed like it was moving backward. It took forever to get to two o'clock. I told Mom I was going to the park. I'm sure she thought I was going to meet Sandra. Me meeting a guy? Inconceivable! I thought about my conversation with Andrew about a million times, trying to figure out if maybe I was making the whole love-thing up and he just wanted to be friends. It was driving me crazy! I'm no good at this! Finally I just left for the park, even though it was way too early. I walked up and down the street next to the park twice, just to kill time. I got to the swings about twenty minutes early. There were some little kids playing on the tire swing, so I sat on the bench. I tried not to be obviously looking for him, but Andrew waved to me as soon as I saw him. I'm obviously not very good at not being obvious.

I started to get more and more nervous as he got closer and closer. He sat down next to me and told me a story about his little brother—how he would only wear his underpants over his regular pants. He said it was driving his mom nuts, but that it was perfectly reasonable. Why would you wear super-cool Spidey underwear under your pants, where no one could see them? It was funny and helped a ton to calm me down.

He asked about my job and the nosy librarian, and the more we talked, the less nervous I got. I even had a moment when I could almost see us on the bench, like I was watching a movie, and I thought, This is perfect! This is great!

When the little kids left the park, Andrew asked if I wanted to sit on the tire swing and eat donuts. I nodded yes because I was still a little unsure about how my voice would come out—squeaky, normal, or desperate sounding. It's almost easier to talk with your mouth full of donut because then at least you have an excuse for sounding weird. It just doesn't look as good. I took little bites so it wouldn't be so gross when I said anything. And then after a while I guess I just forgot to be nervous. Andrew must have thought we'd be starving because he brought a dozen donuts. I could only eat two. When we finished eating, Andrew put the box on the ground next to the bench for the squirrels. I don't know what it is about squirrels, but they are always hungry and ready to eat. You'd think they'd be as fat as little pigs, but they aren't. We had a lot of fun watching a little black squirrel try and decide if he should have a doughnut or not. Andrew did a running commentary like a sportscaster. "He's coming in deep around the end. The end zone's an all clear except for the pigeon. Can he make it?" I don't know anything about sports, but it was funny.

SQUIRREL WITH DONUT

Andrew said he'd always fantasized about having a squirrel for a pet. I said I wasn't crazy about wild animals getting up close, and then I told him about the time my family went to South Dakota and drove through a nature preserve with deer and buffalo and wild burros. The donkeys were so friendly that they came up to the car window looking for apples, and if you didn't give them one, they'd slime the window with their tongues. It was gross and funny at the same time.

Andrew and I were laughing so hard that I didn't see it coming until it almost happened. He was going to kiss me. And then he did it! It was the most amazing kiss ever! I almost fell off the swing, but he put his arm around me to save me. I couldn't help it, I said, "Wow!" It was a totally stupid thing to say but Andrew didn't seem to mind; he just smiled. I guess by now he knows I'm not super cool or even mildly cool. My head was buzzing and I felt tingly all over. It could have been the sugar in the donuts, but I think it was the kiss. We sat on the swing for about another twenty minutes smiling and talking. I can't even explain how fantastic it was.

Suddenly Andrew said, "Oh, man! I've got to go." He said his family was going to his cousin's for two days, and he'd promised his Mom he'd be home by 3:30. I didn't want it to end. Andrew didn't either because he said, "I wish we'd met at 12 instead of 2." And then right when he said 2, I leaned over and kissed him. I didn't even think about it, I just did it! It was so totally not like me. I'm never that brave.

Andrew didn't say something stupid like wow, instead he whispered in my ear. He said, "We'll have to do more of this." It was unbelievably romantic! I wanted to say, Where, when, what time? But I just nodded my head yes. I watched him go and he turned around to wave at me four times before I couldn't see him anymore. If a mom and her two kids hadn't just arrived I would have

yelled, "I LOVE THIS PARK!" I was that happy. The little kids were
excited about all the squirrels eating the donuts. Our black squirrel was still there too.

The mom said she would throw away the donut box before she
left, so I decided to leave. The walk home was completely different. It was like I was on a skateboard or something, just gliding
along. When I walked in the door, Mom said, "You look happy." I
told her I was and that I was going upstairs to call Sandra. She
did her Mom sigh and said, "I don't know what you two girls have
to talk about all the time." It was nice to have everything being
normal and to feel so great. Sandra picked up the phone before
it even really rang. She said she'd been dying and waiting for me
to call. She asked for all the details, but I just gave her a general
rundown. It seemed almost too special to share. I wanted to save
it all for me, and some things are just too hard to describe.
Sandra and I laughed about the tire swing and she renamed it
the "k swing" since Mike had first kissed her there too. I didn't
say anything, but I thought about it being the triple-kiss swing.

She invited me over, but I wanted to keep my afternoon all to myself for a least one more day. Sandra asked if Andrew and I were officially dating. I said, "No one gets a boyfriend that fast, except you and cute girls on sixty-minute TV shows." Besides, knowing Andrew likes me is about all I can take right now. It is perfect.

Chapter 34

MONDAY

TRUTH

TRUE:

I kissed Mike.

I wish it had never happened.

I never told Sandra about it, because I didn't think it would ever matter to her.

TRUTH:

It probably would totally matter to her.

I purposely caught up with Mike at my locker and asked him to come outside and talk with me. I'm not sure if he knew what was up, but he seemed nervous—or it could just have been my nervousness hanging like a fog over both of us. Anyway, I said, "What should we do about the tire thing that happened between us?" I was totally shocked when he said, "Nothing. It has nothing to do with Sandra—it was just a big mistake!" For half a second I was offended to be called a "mistake," but he was right. It was a mistake. I couldn't think of anything else to say so I said, "Okay." So now instead of just my solo pretend-it-didn't-happen secret, I have a real secret. It's more dangerous if Sandra finds out, but there is less danger of her finding out since we are both agreeing not to say anything. I should have felt relieved, but I'm not entirely sure I felt better.

TRUTHFUL: It's something that it is hard to be.

i ate lunch with Sandra and Mike. I could tell that Sandra was happy that we were all doing something together. I wasn't so sure that Mike was right about not telling her about the kisstake. Suddenly I was having a hard time NOT thinking about it. It was the kind of thing that was either going to get bigger or smaller over time. It's hard to say which . . . but, there I was risking it.

IF YOU KNEW STORM CLOUDS WERE ON THE HORIZON, AND YOU COULD BLOW THEM AWAY... WOULDN'T YOU?

I wanted everything to stay good, at least for a little bit, plus tomorrow is Tuesday!!!

FRIENDS

In General

There is no such thing as a perfect-for-you friend, because everything is always changing and no one person can change that fast to fill up all your changing wants, desires, and needs. No one except a superhero, and where am I going to find one of those?

You just have to be happy with the closest you can get.

More complicated means you end up with a huge tangled heap of feelings and loyalties to sort through. A full-time job of remembering who said what, who likes who, who doesn't like what, etc. Seems like a good time to start a journal. Might help me keep it all straight. Maybe.

Mix = COMPLI-CATED LIFE *

* BUT HOPEFULLY YUMMY.

Two more stories about friendship, identity, and surviving— school that is!

click here (to find out
how i survived seventh grade)
By Denise Vega

When Erin's blog is accidentally posted on the school's Intranet, everyone is talking about her pillow-kissing exercises, her frustration with her be friend, her crush on "Cute Boy," and her brother's frog-decorated boxer shor This is one year that Erin will never forget—if she can survive.

The Year of the Dog
Written and illustrated by Grace Lin

It's the Chinese Year of the Dog, and as Pacy celebrates with her family, she learns this is the year she is supposed to "find herself." As the year goes on, she struggles to find her talent, makes a new best friend, and discovers just why the Year of the Dog is a lucky one for her after all.

Little, Brown and Company
Books for Young Readers
Hachette Book Group USA
www.lb-kids.com

Available wherever books are se